Books by Edwin O'Connor

THE ORACLE

THE LAST HURRAH
(*Atlantic Prize Novel, 1955*)

BENJY

THE EDGE OF SADNESS

I WAS DANCING

I
Was
Dancing

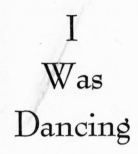

EDWIN O'CONNOR

I
Was
Dancing

An *Atlantic Monthly Press Book*

LITTLE, BROWN AND COMPANY · BOSTON · TORONTO

ATLANTIC–LITTLE, BROWN BOOKS
ARE PUBLISHED BY
LITTLE, BROWN AND COMPANY
IN ASSOCIATION WITH
THE ATLANTIC MONTHLY PRESS

Published simultaneously in Canada
by Little, Brown & Company (Canada) Limited

PRINTED IN THE UNITED STATES OF AMERICA

To Veniette
With Love

I
Was
Dancing

one

IT was Tuesday morning, it was early September. Seven o'clock: outside, the first morning haze of late summer, a slight trembling of the air that was not quite a breeze, silence except for starlings. Old Daniel Considine woke. He woke, simply, by opening his eyes wide. He did not struggle from dreams; he did not dream. He slept soundly every night, without interruption; every morning at this same hour he opened his eyes. He was awake. He lay quietly in his bed, watching the morning, doing nothing, thinking about himself. He was an old man, he knew how to pace himself and in the morning he liked to start slow. He enjoyed nothing more than this first long space of stillness on his bed, making not even the minimum motions of his body, watching the sun edge up the windowpane, and thinking about what mattered. Soon he would move, but not yet; at his age,

he reminded himself, there was no rush about anything. No no, no rush at all. . . .

After a while, the sounds began. They were
small sounds: muffled by thick walls, rugs, oak
flooring, they were barely audible in the room
below, but soft as they were they woke Tom Considine. They woke him every morning, to his
continuing annoyance and surprise. Far louder
sounds, the Great Noises of the city — traffic,
bells, pneumatic drills, the trailing scream of jets
— left him undisturbed; he slept through them
all. It was a simple matter of accommodation, of
getting used to them: two or three nights, no
more. But he had been unable to get used to these
small sounds, these relatively negligible sounds
made every morning by his father, and they had
been going on, not for a few days or weeks, but for
a full year. Every day at this hour the first faint
thuddings overhead caused him to turn uneasily on
his bed, to mumble, stretch, blink, and sigh, and
finally to lie flat on his back — forty-four, thinner
than most, crisp dark hair above the quiet narrow
face — and stare at the ceiling, as if trying to peer
through it into the room above, the source of the
muted reveille.

If he could not see, he could at least imagine:

he had a fair idea of the beginning of what went on up there — although of what happened *after* the beginning he had no idea at all. But he could imagine his father now, sitting on the edge of his bed, alert, watchful, motionless except for the gently tapping foot: six feet tall, still straight, white-topped, almost translucent — a spare old man of seventy-eight, perched there in flashy pajamas. The pajamas had baffled Tom from the first. Otherwise unfailingly severe in his dress — blue-black serges, high collars gleaming with starch, somber socks and funeral ties — his father wore the antic pajamas of a child. They blazed with color: red, green, canary-yellow. All were covered with what Tom at first took for small heraldic symbols, but which on closer inspection proved to be, astonishingly, miniature representations of popular candy bars: Snickers, Mr. Peanut, Charleston Chew. Which meant — what? Anything? Nothing? Tom did not know. Once, quite early in his father's stay — when the two had talked together more — Tom had asked about these pajamas; the old man had answered readily but with that evasive volubility which could be said to be his style; in the end, Tom had learned nothing.

The truth was that his father lived in a nest of

[5]

small and maddening mysteries. Tom knew, for instance, that very soon now the soft tapping would stop, it would be succeeded by footsteps, lightly padding across the floor. Then would follow the other sounds: a window closing, water running, a snatch of song. A shoe would drop, a toilet flush. All normal morning sounds, all sounds of someone getting up for the day. Only — *his father was not getting up for the day.* His father was not getting up at all: whatever the day, he did not rise until noon. So then, why this fake rising? This false start, day after day, which meant nothing and accomplished nothing — except, of course, to snatch the sleeping from their sleep?

It was now exclusively in terms of vexing questions like this that Tom considered his father.

Upstairs, Daniel had already begun his little game. It was a game he played every morning — in a sense, out of respect to the past. Lying on his back, he began slowly to slide his legs across the mattress to the side of the bed, slipping them out from under sheet and blankets — the night had been hot, but Daniel welcomed heat: it was his own belief that as a man grew old the fat of his body evaporated in tiny invisible clouds, leaving

him uninsulated and vulnerable to chills — and gradually pivoting himself around so that when his legs dipped to the floor he would come up into a sitting position without effort or the possibility of strain. He was not a fragile man, but he was not a careless man, either.

He sat on the edge of the bed — just as his son had envisioned him — tapping the floor with one foot, looking down at his legs with admiration. They were long, chalk-white, still smooth and supple: not knots or bunches or big blue veins.

"The old legs," he said, aloud and fondly. "The legs are the thing: when they go, you go."

And of course the whole point was that his legs had *not* gone. They had served him for half a century on stages all over the world; they had not failed him once. They were great legs. He had treated them as such, and they had responded in kind.

"Fair is fair," he said, remembering this. "Oh yes. One good turn deserves another."

And as he sat there, in no particular hurry, looking down at his legs, he began to sing. He sang almost without realizing that he was doing so; it was a part of the morning routine. He sang softly, in a clear and surprisingly sweet tenor, the imperfectly remembered words of a song popular a great many years ago; as he sang, his feet slipped into easy automatic accompaniment on the floor:

Can she bake a cherry pie, Billy boy, Billy boy?
Can she bake a cherry pie, charming Billy?
Dum dee di dum di dee di
Quick as dum dum di your eye,
She's a fine girl but cannot leave her mother. . . .

He had started another chorus when the telephone on his bedside table rang; he answered it immediately. The telephone had been here when he had arrived; it was an extension phone, installed in this bedroom by accident. A lucky accident, he thought, for he was fond of the telephone and used it often. Still, there were times when it was not so lucky, and this was one of them; the call was not for him, but for his son.

"Is Tom there?" a voice said.

"Nobody's awake," Daniel said, and hung up. He was not sure that this was true, but it did not matter. Some time ago he had decided to answer all calls for his son and his daughter-in-law by denying that they were in or available. He did this out of fairness to himself. *Because what the hell am I,* he thought indignantly, *a damn messenger boy? At my age?*

He rose now and stood by the window at the

foot of his bed, looking out into the quiet unoccupied morning, and paying it no attention. With his light, dancer's step he crossed quickly to the bureau, where, in front of the mirror, he stared at himself for thirty seconds or so: old light-blue eyes critically regarding the almost unlined skin. He was satisfied; he nodded and moved slightly to the left, where he stood with his back against the wall. He brushed one hand back across his hair until it touched a small piece of sticking plaster fixed to the wall: he had put the plaster in this spot the night he had arrived, just one year ago. And now, as then, he had met the level with the top of his head. So that in the year he had not bent, he had not shriveled. He knew that old men usually came to this, he had spent much time watching his contemporaries warp and dwindle in their persons, but so far, at least, he was still straight as a string and six feet one.

After this came the next step: the good long morning look at his surroundings. The room was long, white, spare and trim: it might have been a carpenter's version of Daniel himself. He had been in it day and night for a year now, and yet in spite of this the room remained curiously impersonal — almost as if no one had been there at all. This was the effect Daniel had always had on all his rooms.

He had the touch of the transient; in his time, and because of his profession, he had passed through the spectrum of possible accommodations: boardinghouses, barns, barracks, motels, hotels of every grade and description. He had known the medieval splendors of a glum Teutonic castle, his host a demented margrave who was also a vaudeville buff; once out West he had lived a week in a wigwam; in New Zealand, he maintained, he had spent a night inside a hollow stone. But wherever he had stopped, and for however long, he had left his setting as he had found it, and now, although this was entirely different, although at last he was where he meant to be and where he meant to stay, he had not changed his habits. He still impressed himself lightly; the one sign of his long residence here was a large theatrical poster, framed and hung on a side wall:

ONE WEEK ONLY

WALTZING
DANIEL
CONSIDINE!

Apart from this, and a small record player on the bedside table, there seemed to be nothing personal, nothing of his own. Which of course was of some support to his son and his daughter-in-law when, even after his year with them, they still spoke of this room as The Guest Room. At first Daniel had thought this terminology careless; it was only recently that he had come to see it for what it was. It was threatening. He did not care. He had made his plans, and he had great confidence in his own abilities.

He began to move about now, deftly, swiftly, and rather noisily. It was the time of morning when he went through the main part of his little game, performing a kind of rite which had been far more than a rite in the old days. For on a great many days of his long professional life he had risen very early indeed; he had been given no choice. At the mercy of whimsical booking agents and maniac travel schedules, he had spent more mornings than he could remember rising well before dawn, stumbling and cursing around a strange room in a strange town, splashing a bit of water on his face, jumping into his clothes, throwing his few possessions into the one suitcase — he had always required few props, he had always traveled light — and then rushing, still fogged with sleep, down the stairs and into the lobby and out onto the street where a taxi might — but might not — be on hand to take him to the bus, which would in turn deposit him at four o'clock in the morning at some desolate junction where, shaking in the darkness and blue with the cold, he would wait for the train which would bring him to the split-week booking in Valparaiso, Indiana. Or Cardiff, Wales. Or Woonsocket, Rhode Island. Or Paris, France.

As an old vaudevillian, he had had fifty years of this, and he did not regret it. Instead, he had loved it, all of it; even the miseries were softened in memory. So that in a way it had been a great life, and now that it was over he looked back on it with satisfaction, fondness, and some complacency. For Vaudeville was dead — but he was not. He paid the deceased the tribute of the loving and slightly indulgent survivor: he pretended, for a few minutes each day, that it was still alive, and that he was still with it. And so every morning he got out of bed at this early hour and zigzagged full tilt — or at what passed for full tilt with him these days — around the room, making all the movements and sounds exactly as he used to. It was Daniel in his private game. Or not quite private,

for these sounds were audible in other parts of the
house, but Daniel had no time to be bothered about
that. He was busy making believe that in just a
matter of minutes now he would be hustling from
the room and down the stairs and out into the
morning, there to begin still another freezing,
broken-backed journey into the heart of the Gus
Sun time.

It was at this point that he went back to bed.
He had enjoyed himself, but the game was over:
enough was enough. He was a sentimental man,
but he was a practical one, too: he reminded himself often that what a man his age needed above
all else was plenty of rest. It was for this reason
that he stayed in bed each day until noon. He was
not tired, but he owed it to himself to take care.
He rested in bed, then, spending his time pleasantly, telephoning to old friends, listening to a few
of the good old songs on his record player, and
reading. He read mostly about himself. Under his
bed he kept a pile of large, fat, green-colored scrapbooks. They had traveled all over the world with
him and, taken together, they constituted a history
of sorts: Fifty Years of Waltzing Daniel Considine.
It was the only history that really interested him;
he read it over and over, morning after morning.

Sometimes he focused on a single year; sometimes
he read anywhere and anything, skipping back
and forth among the decades. Sometimes he read
only the rave notices; sometimes he even read those
where he had been treated harshly. There were
only a few of these, and he could read them now
with only the faintest flicker of the old anger; for
the most part he was amused, forgiving.

"The poor silly bastards," he said.

On the whole, it made little difference to him
what he read; in all newsprint about himself he
now found comfort, refreshment, and reward.

It was the way he spent his mornings. He rose
at noon, slowly dressed, went downstairs, said
hello (politely), had a bit of food, and received
any of his old friends who dropped in to see him.
Occasionally, if the weather was good, he went for
a short walk. In the evenings, if another old friend
or two happened by, he sat up for a while to talk,
but never for very long: since he rose (in a manner of speaking) early, he liked to be in bed at a
decent hour.

Of his son and his daughter-in-law, technically
his host and hostess, he saw increasingly little. As
the weeks had passed, somehow it seemed that he
and they had less and less to say to each other. In

a way, Daniel thought, it was a pity. Not because he missed what they might say to him — God knows he had never found *that* very interesting: dull stuff, all about themselves — but because if they had listened properly he could have told them much. Still, he reflected, it was just as well: he could have used up all his time talking away to them; it would have been a dreadful waste. Sometimes he had a vision in which his son and his daughter-in-law sat with him, not as they were in fact, but as they might have been: in this vision they sat open-mouthed on the forward edge of the living room love seat while he talked on and on about long-ago triumphs and the wonders he had seen. It was a vision he always found ultimately exasperating, and quite often he would shout aloud, "For the love of God, let me be! I can't waste all day like this! I've got things of my own to do! What the hell am I, an old man or a Victrola?"

The sound of his own voice always brought him out of this; blinking, he knew that he had been dozing, or close to it. So then, his son and his daughter-in-law had not usurped his time; he had been unjust to them; a fair man, he now made amends by speaking of them more generously.

"I'll say this for them," he said. "They're a damn queer pair, the two of them. . . ."

Below, his son was dressing. As usual, once awakened, he could not get back to sleep, and the result had been that once more he had risen considerably earlier than he had planned. He had bathed and shaved to the beat of his father's upstairs caperings, shaking his head over the absurdity of it all. Midway through the process the telephone had rung; still wet, he had hurried to answer it, but he was too late — as he knew he would be. Freshly exasperated, he could not help an unwilling admiration at the old man's agility. He was — what? Seventy-six? Seventy-seven? Seventy-eight? And still leaping. . . .

And yet it could not have been allowed to continue. Talk was no good; in recent weeks — for the past month — his father had not talked to them at all. But in Tom's mind was the larger question of whether he had *ever* talked to them, or they to him. Was conversation with his father possible? In those early months, when he had sat across from his father in the living room at night, curious, eager to pick up threads, he had found it an altogether unsatisfying business. There had been no shortage of words — words and words and words — but there had been no bridge, no connection. His father had not talked *all* the time; occasionally he had listened, politely and with every appearance of attention — and then, slowly, he swam back into the great stream of his own reminiscence, untouched by Tom, immune to everything he said.

No, he could not talk with his father. Could anyone? Apparently so: his father was not without visitors. They were mostly his contemporaries; they came to see him often and stayed a long time; presumably, then, they talked. But about what? Tom had been given a clue to this one day during the summer. He had picked up the telephone in the downstairs hall, only to discover that his father was already using the invaluable bedroom extension. After hesitating just slightly, and feeling the minimum amount of shame, Tom, curious, had eavesdropped.

". . . you take heat," his father was saying. "I like heat but yesterday was too damn hot. I didn't go out but I knew it was going to be a scorcher the minute I woke up in the morning."

"All records were smashed to smithereens yesterday, Daniel," the other voice said. Tom recognized it: Billy Ryan. He was a short, untidy, pigeon-shaped man with bulging eyes and an important manner; younger than Daniel by some twenty years, he seemed nevertheless to belong to his world. He was a physician. (Or was he? There was always a doubt, Tom thought, about all his father's friends.) "You were much better off in the privacy of your cool room. You could hang meat in that room, my dear man."

"Yes," Daniel said, "the moment I opened my eyes I said to myself, 'Well, Daniel, the streets will be boiling by noon.' And they were. I can always tell about heat before it happens. I dunno how I can, but I can."

"There's a medical explanation for that, my dear man. Scientifically speaking, we call it the Inborn Talent. It's something you can't pick up for yourself, no matter how hard you try. *It's something you have to be born with.*"

"They were keeling over from the heat yesterday," Daniel said. "On the street, right in front of the house. I was at the window, watching them go down. By God, they were dropping like flies!"

"Inevitable, Daniel. The day being what it was. Medically speaking, conditions were ideal. The blazing sun, the high humidity — dehydration sets in, and boom!"

"Boom and you're on your arse," his father said.

"Right you are, my dear man! In the language of the layman, boom and you're on your behind. I'll give you my professional advice for days like this, Daniel: have plenty of salt with you at all times. We can learn from the beasts of the fields on that one."

"I don't need to take lessons from animals," Daniel said. "Anyways, I don't go out. Not these days. I know damn well when it's going to be hot."

"A precious gift, my dear man. And mysterious as well. Medical science knows about it, yes, but we don't know *all* about it. Even the best of us can't say why all of a sudden some little part comes unglued in somebody before he's out of his mother's womb, and the result is an Einstein or a Samson. Or yourself. A mathematical genius, the strongest man in the world, and a human barometer. Think that over, Daniel. There's a mystery for you!"

"Oh yes," Daniel said. "I tell you, when it comes to heat, I'm the boy to talk to. You can keep your weathermen."

"Some of the finest weathermen of my acquaintance," said Billy, "have been very poor on heat. . . ."

Tom had hung up softly. For the first time he

wondered if his father might not be senile. He had
mentioned this to his wife; she had dismissed the
possibility with a look. On second thought, he had
agreed with her. Some years younger than Tom
— fair-haired, fresh-faced, with great gray eyes —
she was inclined to trust rather than to suspect,
but almost from the first she had been wary of his
father. One night, quite early in old Daniel's stay
here, in fact, Tom had felt her move in bed — he
had supposed her to be asleep — and suddenly her
arms had been tight around him, and she had
whispered, her lips brushing his ear, "But don't
you *see*? He's wearing a mask, twenty-four hours
a day! He's really a very clever old man!"

And there had been those times during the year
when Tom had been sitting alone with his father,
listening perhaps none too carefully as the old
man drifted along in his monologue, when for
some reason something in his father's voice —
some overtone, some little intonation — would
give him the sudden feeling that if he were to lift
his head, very quickly, and look directly at this
moment into his father's eyes, he would encounter, not the familiar, mild, old-blue gaze, but a
stare of freezing calculation. He never did, but
the feeling remained. . . .

For the past week, during his wife's absence —
visiting her sister, she would be flying back tomorrow — Tom had thought of little else but his father: that strange old man whom, for so many
years, he had not seen at all, and whom, for the
past year, he had seen every day. Each day had
brought with it something new in the way of mystery, annoyance, farce. Even the manner of his father's arrival had been purest farce: the doorbell
at midnight; Tom, stumbling half-asleep down the
stairs; opening the door and finding there — a
stranger. Who, two seconds later, turned out to be
his father. Characteristic, he thought wryly: others
get foundlings on their doorsteps. I get my father.

The old man had come in "for a minute"; he was
here still. The days had simply slipped into each
other, and his father had slipped in with them. It
had all happened easily, imperceptibly, incredibly
— so that quite literally Tom had awakened one
morning to realize, with astonishment and exasperation, that the overnight transient had some
time ago become a feature in his home. He and
his wife were reluctant hosts to a persisting guest
— a guest, moreover, who in some mysterious way
seemed to impinge upon their lives as he disappeared from their view. For the longer he stayed

the less visible he became: even before the meeting, the "showdown," of a month ago, he had begun to keep to himself and to his room, as if following some master plan. They saw him seldom, but they were aware of him as never before: unfilially, Tom compared his father to some as-yet-unclassified burrowing mammal, old and cunning, his tiny paws tunneling out for himself private spaces within the larger compound, his presence betrayed by small mounds of earth and subterranean whistles.

Overhead, the shoe dropped. Tom winced and glanced automatically at his watch. He saw that, as usual, his father was punctual. Even today, he thought, even today of all days, he's right on the button. . . .

But there was a difference today. In his room, Daniel had come to a stop and now was standing still in the center of the floor. This morning, for the first time in months, he was not returning to his bed; from the moment he woke, and all through his little game, he remembered very well just what this particular day was, and its special relevance to him. He could not afford to go back to bed and take it easy; not today. Today he expected to be busy. Very busy.

"All the damn day long," he said, "and half the nighttime, too! It's a hell of a thing for an old man!"

But he did not seem entirely displeased; suddenly he broke into a quick little clog step to indicate his readiness for anything that might come along.

"Oh yes!" he said. "The bite of the snake, but I'll show them a thing or two!"

He began now to get ready for the day. Laying out his sedate public clothes with care, stripping off his Mr. Peanut pajamas, he washed, shaved, hurried back and forth to the mirror now and then to take a good look at himself, and every once in a while he sang a snatch of good old "Billy Boy." He talked to himself frequently; because he had spent so much of his life alone, it was a habit of long standing. All in all, it took him some time to get dressed; then he sat in the chair by the window to go over in detail the plans he had spent the past month perfecting in preparation for this day.

Somewhat later, his son, before leaving for his office, came up, paused before his father's door, and knocked. He did this every morning.

"Dad?" he called.

Daniel heard both the knock and the call, but as

usual he did not answer. He sat there, waiting for what came next.

"All right," his son said crisply. "I just wanted to tell you I'm leaving now. If you need anything, Annie's here."

If I need anything, Daniel thought grimly: *aren't you the good fairy?* But for a moment he was startled; he had thought — and hoped — that his son's wife was still away. Then, relieved, he remembered that Annie was the name of the girl who came in to clean; the wife's name was . . . what? Ellen. He knew this, to be sure, and yet, since he thought of her and spoke of her only as "the wife," it was sometimes hard to remember.

He heard the door slam; he stood by the window, watching his son walk down the street. He saw in his walk something he had noticed before; it reminded him of long ago.

"His mother," he said. "He's got a walk like his mother."

Old Daniel had not in fact spent much time with his wife, but he remembered her quite well.

two

IN mid-morning, Daniel had his first caller of the day. He had been in his chair for a long time, thinking; now he had risen and was standing by the window, looking out at nothing in particular, when the knock came. He turned to face the door, but did not move towards it; he appeared to be waiting. After a moment the knock was repeated, but this time as if it were a kind of signal: one long, three shorts. Old Daniel walked quickly to the door, opened it, and said, "Come in, Billy. Come into the cell."

"Right you are, my dear man," Billy Ryan said. "Right with Eversharp."

He came in with the bustling movements of a busy little fat man; Daniel said, "What does that mean?"

"What does what mean, my dear man?"

"That right with Eversharp."

"A slogan on a radio show years ago. I say it occasionally out of habit. We're all creatures of habit, Daniel. But it means nothing. A phrase of insignificance. Like 'How are you?' or 'One, two, button my shoe.' That kind of thing."

"Well," Daniel said, "I suppose it makes as much sense as most of the stuff you hear nowadays, anyways. Sit down, Billy. Have a chair."

"Thank you, my dear man, I will with pleasure. With the old *avec plaisir*, as the French put it." He carried a black physician's satchel; he flipped this onto the bed with a surprising nonchalance and then fell plumply into a chair. "I've had an exhausting morning, my dear man. With a patient who's passing away by the minute." Examining his wristwatch, he said professionally, "She may very well be dead now."

Curious about death, Daniel asked, "Who is she? Anyone I'd know?"

"No no, my dear man. Personally unknown to us all. A poor old woman whose bones are slowly turning to jelly. The precise disease defies my diagnosis. I was called in too late. Well, how are you, my dear man?"

"All right," Daniel said. "I didn't know it was

you the first time when you knocked. Did you use the special knock?"

"My apologies, Daniel. I was so professionally preoccupied I completely forgot the necessity for the code."

"It's a damn silly thing, I suppose, when you come right down to it: a man my age having a password knock to the door of his own room. But by God if I didn't have it, you know what would happen. It'd be allee allee in free to the whole damn world."

"A man's home is his castle, Daniel, no matter how big or how small. And this room is your home."

"You're damn right it is," Daniel said grimly. "No matter what some people think."

"Could I put it this way, Daniel?" Billy said. "Have there been any late developments?"

Daniel shook his head. "No. Nothing new. I —" He stopped suddenly, and raised a warning hand to Billy; he cocked his head and listened. As old as he was, he had sharp ears; he had often observed that none of the callers who came to this room could hear the things he could. It was a matter for congratulation: sight, taste, sound, smell, all good, all in order. . . .

The knock came. It was not the code knock, but two light and rather timid raps. Daniel motioned Billy to keep silence, and waited; the knock came again, now slightly bolder.

"I'm in here being examined by my personal physician!" Daniel said loudly. "You'll have to wait! Come back tomorrow!"

There was no further sound; Billy said, "Well well, my dear man: they keep it up, I see. You're living in what might be called, scientifically speaking, a virtual state of siege. Who would that have been? Tom's wife, no doubt?"

"No," Daniel said. "The wife's away. Until tomorrow. At least that's what she's supposed to be. For all I know she may still be here, hiding in a room somewheres, spying on people and minding their business. No, that was the maid. A poor little Canuck nitwit that comes in to tidy up now and then. She was already in once today to make up the bed. I let her in because she's harmless, but I watch her all the same."

"Prudent, my dear man, prudent. Otherwise the door is closed to all comers?"

"That's right. Except my friends: yourself, Gottlieb, Father Feeley, and one or two more. And my sister Delia: I let her in every once in a while. God

knows why, but I do. But the rest I keep out. Even
my own son. Even Tom. I hate like hell to do that
to my own boy."

"And in his own house, too," Billy said.

"I hate like hell to do that to my own boy, Billy,
because I'm a great family man. The only reason
I came back was to be with what's left of my family. My own boy. And it was the damnedest thing
— the way I came back, I mean. Have I told you
this before, Billy?"

"You've mentioned it, my dear man," Billy said,
"from time to time."

"There I was," Daniel said reflectively, "one year
ago yesterday. Flat on my back in the Blue Devil
Motel, out in Pasadena, California. Not sick, you
know, but a little tired: I'd been out playing a benefit for the Veterans of Foreign Wars. God knows
why, it was one of those things a man gets sucked
in on now and then. Anyways, there I was, lying
there, looking up at the ceiling, the way you do
when you're thinking of different things and can't
go to sleep right away. And all of a sudden it came
to me. Out of the blue! It was like a voice in the
same room with me saying, 'Go home, Daniel!
You've had it all: go home.'"

"That's a very frequent occurrence throughout

medical history, my dear man: the inside voice saying, 'Hello there.' Look at Saint Joan of Arc."

"You look at her," Daniel said, shortly. "I'm looking at Waltzing Daniel Considine. Well, anyways, I said to myself, 'I sure as hell don't know what it is, but by God, it makes sense. I damn well will go home!' And I did. The very next day I was on a jet plane. First class. By God, Billy, I keep on thinking I've told you this before."

"Never mind that, my dear man," Billy said. "It's a very moving story on any occasion."

"Well," Daniel said, "to make a long story short, when I got to town it was night. I picked up my bag at the airport and took a taxicab here to Tom's house straightaway. I got here at a quarter to twelve midnight. I rang the bell and it was Tom that answered. In his pajamas. And when he saw who it was, standing there, he damn near died."

"Father and son, reunited at last!" Billy said. He had heard the story before but, once caught up in it, he succumbed eagerly to its drama and even helped it along. "The boy was no doubt overcome with joy, Daniel?"

"*Surprised* is what he was mainly, I think. He'd had no word I was coming, you see. And then, of course, it was some time since I'd come home last." He nodded and said thoughtfully, "Twenty-one years."

"Twenty-one years!" Billy said. "What we might call, my dear man, a substantial interval."

"I suppose," Daniel said. "Anyways, that's what he was to see me: surprised."

"And the wife, Daniel?" Billy said. "There would have been an element of surprise there as well? If my information is correct, she'd never even set eyes on you before?"

"That's right," Daniel said. "The two of them got married while I was away. So I never knew her. And she never knew me. But what the hell difference did that make? It wasn't her I came back to see, it was Tom. To see and to stay with. And why not? Where else would I come if not to my own boy's house?"

"The logical terminus, my dear man."

"So he was a little surprised to see me, you know, but he was glad, too. There's no reason why he shouldn't of been. I'm his father. We were always friendly enough. I don't say we were pals, exactly, but that's because I was away so much. I was always away a good bit, Billy. On tour."

"That's the way of the entertainer, Daniel," Billy said. "Every profession has its harsh necessities.

The interrupted sleep is mine; I frequently get calls in the middle of the night."

"So what the hell," Daniel said, "it started out all right. And now I can't even let him into my room. I've had to keep him out for a whole month now, and it's only tonight I can let him in."

Billy said, "Tonight's the deadline, I believe?"

"It's the deadline, all right. By God, Billy, just think of it!" In sudden indignation he rose and stood dramatically in front of his old friend. "To-night, Billy, I'm supposed to get out of this house. Out of it for good! How d'ye like that, Billy? The walking papers! Slipped to me by my own son! There's family feeling for you!"

"Shakespeare has a line about that one, Daniel," Billy said. "I forget it for the moment, but it's there."

"O-u-t spells out: out for Waltzing Daniel Con-sidine! Oh, they put it nice as pie, but that's what they meant, all right. It's the wife that's behind it, of course. Tom by himself would of done nothing. He hasn't the spunk. But the wife: there's a tricky one, Billy. All smiles and blonde hair and sugar-plums, you know, when she sits there with her hands in her lap. But underneath, bing, bang, biff: watch out for the tiger!"

"The female of the species, Daniel. Medically speaking, they're all alike. Look at the famous Greek, Helen of Troy."

"Oh by God!" cried Daniel. "Wouldn't she of liked to get in here, though! To get in here and start clearing my stuff out. First my stuff, and then me. That's the way she had it planned. Well, she can damn well change her plans. Because my stuff's not going, Billy. And I'll tell you something else: *neither am I*. This is where I want to stay, and this is where I'm going to stay. And I can promise you that!"

Billy did not dissent; he said only, "I applaud your resolution, my dear man. . . ."

Much earlier, Tom had decided to walk to the office: he had time, it was little more than a mile, and besides, on this day, he thought he needed much time alone. The walk was a good one, but the route was a mistake. He had just turned off the Boulevard, and was approaching the great gray pile of Saint Monica's Church, when he saw, edging along, old Father McGovern. This pious, tiny — five feet three — old man had been pastor of Saint Monica's for a very long time, and now was semi-retired. He had baptized Tom, he had given him his First Communion, he had known him all his life; it was with some feeling of guilt, therefore, that Tom now avoided him whenever possible. For just a second he thought he had succeeded in doing so this morning, but the tree was too small, and the old man, spotting him, waved and hurried over. He had a curious way of appearing to move sideways, his left shoulder slightly in advance of the rest of him, as if he were battling gales.

"Well well, Bob!" he said, in his startling voice. For from this diminutive man came the sound of a, giant — a sound, moreover, which the years had deepened rather than diminished. This voice was a point of pride with Father McGovern; however large the church or hall, he would no more have used a microphone than he would have worn a dress. "Bob, how are you?"

The "Bob" was not a constant; in his rare conversations with the priest, Tom was sometimes "Bill," sometimes "Fred," sometimes "Jim"; once, and for nearly a year, he had been "Carl." There was no pattern to any of this; Tom had heard — and believed — that the old man never really forgot anyone or anything, but that long ago he had found names unimportant. He said, "I'm well, Father. And yourself?"

"Eighty-three," Father McGovern said. "Eighty-three on Thursday. That answers your question, I think, Bob."

It didn't, really, but neither did it matter; Tom offered his congratulations. The old priest did not acknowledge these but stood in silence, still sideways, peering expectantly over his left shoulder at Tom. So something more was required — but what? Reaching, Tom said, "You never seem to change, Father. You might still be sixty."

But this was a failure — at least, it was not what the old man had been waiting for. He said only, "I was thinking of you on Friday last, Bob. When poor Art Farrell died. He was in your class, I believe. A tall lad with red hair."

Tom knew whom he meant. He had not seen him for years, but he *had* been in school with him, and the man *had* died, very suddenly, one day last week. His name in fact had been Anthony Devlin. He said, "Yes, a sad death. . . ."

"A very BEAUTIFUL death!" roared the old man. "He was a stupid boy and he was a stupid man and he had a sad life, *but he died a beautiful death.* I was with him when he died. I taught you both your catechism. 'Who made the world?' 'God made the world.' First beginnings, eh, Bob?"

"First beginnings, Father." He glanced quickly

up the street. Fortunately it was early, and only one man could be seen — coming along, but still far up and on the other side.

"Poor Art," said the priest. "He always knew the answers. But parrot-fashion. It failed to sustain him in later life. He married very badly, of course. No children. You're married yourself now, Bob?"

"Yes, I'm married, Father." He began to edge away; the tiny man edged with him.

"Six years now, is it?"

"Seven, Father." He changed course slightly but swiftly, taking two steps to the left, hoping in this quick maneuver to get *around* the priest, but Father McGovern pivoted with a sudden adroitness so that he now stood with his right shoulder in the lead, almost touching Tom and blocking further advance.

"Seven," Father McGovern said. "Of course, yes. Seven. And how many children, Bob? Two? Or is it three?"

He was caught; he knew it; the only question was how bad it would be. He saw now that people were coming along the street, several of them; he reflected bitterly that this was all his own fault for having forgotten this old man's habit of morning walks. He said very quickly, "We have no children, Father. And now I have to hurry; I'm late —"

"NO CHILDREN! AFTER SEVEN YEARS OF MAR-
RIAGE!"

It was as bad, worse, than he had expected. The
great cry boomed into space, bouncing off side-
walks, buildings, rooftops; too, with the old man's
peculiar off-center stance, he faced and appeared
to directly address the passers-by who were now
approaching. All looked, some smiled; Tom had
the certainty that he was a figure in some terrible
neighborhood comedy which was re-enacted each
morning.

"Good God, boy!" the priest said, his voice slid-
ing into his pulpit whisper, which was at once
more intimate and more penetrating than his
shout. "Where's your training? Eh? *We can't live
like pagans, Bob!*"

It was fantastic, he thought: thirty-five years
later he was back in the Sunday school classroom:
a child confronted by a bellowing madman, himself no bigger than a child. Desperately he did
what he should have done earlier; he reached
out and grabbed the priest's hand, pumping it
hurriedly. "Goodbye, Father," he said. "I'm very
late —"

But the priest held on tightly for a moment; surprisingly, and in a normal voice, he said, "How's
your father, Bob?"

[37]

"Fine, very well." He was grateful for the change, but he was determined to get away. He pulled his hand, suddenly and hard, and almost fell over backwards, for just as he pulled the old man released him.

"A great entertainer," Father McGovern said. "I've seen him many times. He brought happiness to millions. But that doesn't excuse him from coming to Mass. Give your father my regards, Bob, and tell him to come to Mass." His voice was growing loud again; sternly he said, "He has an obligation there!"

But Tom, waving without looking back, was already moving quickly down the street. He was aware of people as they passed him; he knew there were, there *had* to be, amused glances. He began to walk faster, and just before he turned the far corner to a kind of safety, to at least an immunity from the universal smirk, he heard, catching up with him, enclosing him, sailing past him, the final awful whoop of Father McGovern:

"He has his obligation, Bob! AND YOU HAVE YOURS!"

It was not until much later that morning that he could begin to consider the dreadful meeting with a measure of calm. More farce, he thought;

if it had happened to someone else, he would have thought it funny. He even acknowledged that it had a certain appropriateness to this particular day. His father, Father McGovern — the two men were not unlike. An encounter with either was not an easy matter; neither could be defended against by any of the standard rational procedures. It was in part of course a question of age. Not until recently had Tom thought much about old age; now — or so it seemed to him — he thought about it all the time. He was suddenly surrounded by it; it seemed to him he met a new old man every day; he had begun to realize that old age was a strange and usually hostile world, whose ways and weapons he did not understand at all. This bothered him because now he had to deal with it in the deepest, most personal way. He was not happy about this, but he knew he had no choice: what he was about to do, he knew he had to do, and that was that. And he knew just what he was going to say and do; the trouble was he could not say the same about his father. Tom knew he had the upper hand, he knew that, whatever the old man did, he could not get his way, and yet. . . .

And yet. . . .

He suddenly realized that by yet another route

— the embarrassing lunatic route of Father Mc-
Govern — he had come back to the consideration
of his father. All roads led to Daniel. . . . .

In the house, Daniel was leisurely reviewing his
past.

"Always on tour, Billy. I don't think there's a
theater, big or small, I haven't played, one time or
another. And do you know the reason for that? *I
was in demand.*"

"You were always a very popular artist, Daniel,"
Billy said. "When the history of American vaude-
ville is written, your name will be more than
Among Those Present."

"I was always in demand," Daniel said, dream-
ily. "And not only here. Abroad as well. I was a
big hit in Australia, Billy. I went to Australia twice.
The first time I was there for nearly a year; the
second time I was held over for two. That's how
much I was in demand in Australia."

"I knew you spent some time Down Under,
Daniel. A fascinating part of the world, I'm told."

"The very best. They come no better than Australia. I played the whole country, up and down. I
played the big cities: Melbourne, Perth, Sydney,
Brisbane. I played the small cities and the little

towns, too. I played places you never dreamed of, Billy. I once played a town by the name of Too-woomba. How do you like that for the name of a place? Hey? Toowoomba!"

"It has a very primitive sound, my dear man. In a town with a name like that, I imagine the medical facilities would be at a minimum."

"I dunno," Daniel said. "I was never sick. All the times I was in Australia, I never had so much as a headache. It was grand. Everything was grand; even the traveling around was grand. Oh, I tell you, Billy!"

He leaned back in his chair, his eyes closed, his voice slow and drowsy with remembered pleasures. "You'd pull out of a town, you know, after your week was up, on a kind of a dwarf train and you'd ride for miles and miles, and maybe you wouldn't see anything at all but a few sheep and a jackrabbit. Then all of a sudden you'd pull up in the midst of a place that was hardly a place at all: just a few little sheds and a backhouse. But they'd have their theater, Billy. It wasn't much but they'd have it. And I'd play it. I'd play it twice a day, and in they'd come from miles around. They'd ride horseback in to see me. Half the time I'd be the only act on the bill. There'd be a movie, and there'd be me. No dressing room, no stagehands, nothing. I'd go to the theater, pull the curtain myself so they could see the screen, and the movie would start. Then when it was over I'd drop the curtain, the music would start, and I'd come on. I always made a great entrance, Billy. I always made a great entrance for my act."

"I remember the entrance, Daniel," Billy said. "Medically speaking, the effect was hypnotic."

"I got their eye, if that's what you mean," Daniel said. "By God I did! And right away. No matter how many times they'd seen me before, the heads would snap back. It was all in the way it was done, you know. In the big theaters there'd be the orchestra, of course, but in the little ones I'd have my Victrola along. No matter which, I'd always have the music up good and loud before I came on." He stood now, and went over to his bedside table; turning back to Billy, he explained, "The theme song, you know. All over the world, Billy, as soon as they heard it, they knew it was me."

He reached for the record player and, turning a switch, listened attentively until the music came up. The record was an old one — thin, squeezed, full of scratches — but the melody was clear enough: it was the waltz "Two Hearts Beat in

Three-Quarter Time." As it started, Daniel waved his hands lightly in tempo; over the music he said, "And then, Billy, after a few bars, just to get them all *expecting*, out I'd come, full tilt, you know, whirling out of the wings, white tie and tails, waltzing and singing the way I used to!"

And now the old dancer bent his body slightly forward, held out his arms as if taking a partner, and began to twirl across the room in a Viennese waltz. He was still graceful; it was not hard to believe that he had been a very skilled performer indeed. As he danced, he sang, the clear, almost young tenor going over the words he had sung for so many years:

I'll tell you who's a friend of mine —
He's Waltzing Daniel Considine!
Dum dee, dum dee, dum dum dee dum
Dum dum dee dum di dum
Dum dum dee di dee, dee dum dum dee di
Dum dum dee di dee, dum dum dee di. . . .

And his voice trailed off as, circling the room, he whirled his way back to the table, picked up the needle, and the music abruptly stopped. Daniel made a little bow in Billy's direction.

[43]

"Oh marvelous, my dear man, marvelous!" Billy said. "It's always a pleasure and a privilege to watch you do the light fantastic."

"Oh, I tell you, Billy, those were the great days!" Daniel said. "Waltzing Daniel Considine. I was a big hit everywhere."

"Golden memories, my dear man. They give succor and support to us all. We have plenty of scientific evidence for that."

Daniel shrugged. "But, what the hell, it's all over now. Vaudeville died years ago, but even if it didn't, it wouldn't mean anything to me today. I wouldn't set foot again on a stage if I could. I'm an old man now, Billy. I've worked all my life and I've traveled all my life. You've never met a man that's traveled more than me. But that's all done now. It was all done a year ago when I packed my bag in California and came back home. For good."

"One whole year ago!" Billy said. "My my, Daniel, time goes through us like a dose of salts. That's what they call Relativity. Tell me, my dear man, on the whole you'd say the year has met with your approval, would you?"

"It was all right up till this nonsense started. In the beginning Tom was fine, and even the wife was nice and polite. Later, when she began to get a little chilly around the edges, I didn't mind. I paid no attention to her. I said to myself, 'She can live her life, and I'll live mine. To hell with her.'"

"You don't find that kind of tolerance in everyone, my dear man," Billy said.

"Well, you damn well don't find it in her. She was always fussing around, trailing after me, picking up things, getting in my way. She began to tell me little stories, all about how nice it must be someplace else this time of year. Or else she'd say how dull it must be for me, staying here in the house after all the excitement I had in my life. Hints, you know. Like I was some sort of half-cracked child that couldn't see what she was driving at."

"Women are strange, Daniel," Billy said. "Biologically speaking, they're among the most inscrutable creatures we know."

"And then, Billy," Daniel said, his voice rising, "it happened. One month ago tonight, at the table downstairs. They sat there, side by side, the two of them, and told me. They decided, they said. And what did they decide? They decided it was o-u-t for Waltzing Daniel Considine. Only they didn't put it like that, of course. Oh no! The way they put it, it was all for my own good. The way they put it, it was Christmas Eve, and I was a kid getting nuts in my stocking! Oh yes! They were thinking of *me*, you understand. And all the while Tom did the talking, sitting there like a ventriloquist's dummy, with her beside him not even moving her lips!"

"That was the occasion, was it," Billy asked, "when the Smiling Valley was first suggested?"

"That's right! Oh, they were clever. They said they knew I was tired of hotels and boarding-houses, that what I needed now was a home where I could see lots of people my own age and get good care if I needed it. That was when Tom brought up the Smiling Valley. Good God Almighty! Old as I am, I damn near knocked him down! Waltzing Daniel Considine in an Old Man's Home!"

"Not an Old Man's Home, my dear man," Billy said reprovingly. "They don't call them that any more. And some of them are highly delightful places."

"I don't give a damn what they call them," Daniel said. "They've all got fancy names nowadays. Do you know what the full name of the Smiling Valley is? Saint Vincent's Smiling Valley for Senior Citizens! What the hell kind of nonsense is that? I —"

He broke off sharply as he had once before, and

again held up his hand for silence. He listened for a moment, then, cautiously, he rose and stole over to the door and suddenly pulled it open, at the same time saying loudly, "Well, who is it?"

There was no answer; no one stood there. Daniel stuck his head out into the hall and looked up and down, then came back into the room, carefully closing the door behind him.

"Who was that, my dear man?" Billy said.

"Nobody, that time," Daniel said. "But you never know. I thought I heard someone. And she might of been there, sneaking around; she might of come back early. By God, I don't want them to hear my plans, I can tell you that! Well . . . where was I?"

"The Smiling Valley was the topic, my dear man."

"Yes, well, I know all about that place. That's where my sister Delia lives these days, and she can damn well have it."

"As it happens, Daniel," Billy said, "I'm very familiar with the Smiling Valley. I keep tabs on them all for professional reasons. Don't sell the Smiling Valley short, my dear man. It's very modern, very progressive. With a lovely big lawn and all the latest facilities. And a highly distinguished clientele. I believe Sunny Jo Riordan, the former flyweight boxing champ, is in residence out there at the present time."

"Well, I'll tell you who won't be in residence out there at the present time or any other time," Daniel said, "and that's Waltzing Daniel Considine. I know those Smiling Valleys. A bowl of thin soap in the mouth and a thermometer up the behind twice a day. And everybody out there shuffling around, all held together with Scotch tape and piano wire. What the hell's wrong with you, Billy, thinking I'd go to a place like that?"

"It was just a thought, my dear man. In case the happy home life here didn't come up to snuff."

"Well, it's a thought you can forget about," Daniel said grumpily. "And damn quick, too. I'm going nowhere. I'm staying right here."

"I'm behind you all the way, Daniel," Billy said. "And yet, my dear man, am I right in this: they think you *are* going?"

Daniel nodded. "They do. And they think so because I told them I would. What the hell else was I going to do? They had me over a barrel, the two of them. I can't go when and where I please. I've got no money these days. I made plenty in my time, but one way or another, you know, it went.

So I had to think fast, Billy. I had to use my head. So I said, 'All right, if that's what you want, I'll go. And to the Smiling Valley at that.' "

"Shrewd, Daniel," Billy said approvingly. "Shrewd. Professionally speaking, that's what's known as tactics."

" 'I'll go,' I said," Daniel continued, " 'and you can make the arrangements as soon as you want. One month from tonight I'll leave this house. And I won't come back.' And then, Billy, I looked at them and I said, 'Only don't expect me to come down and join you again. Not after a thing like that. I'll stay in my room, the rest of the time I'm here!' And then I looked at them again — slow, you know — and I left. I came up to my room and I've been here ever since."

"A month in here, Daniel!" Billy exclaimed. "Without ever leaving it once!"

"That's right."

"Except of course for the necessaries," Billy pointed out.

"Yes, well, that's right next door," Daniel said, "and I'm in and out of there like a flash. But as far as Tom and the wife go, I don't see them, and they don't see me. It's all a part of my plan. Waltzing Daniel Considine's going to no Old Man's Home. I

[49]

like it here, Billy. And no matter what any sweet little thing says, this is where I'm going to stay."

"I'm with you there, Daniel," Billy said enthusiastically. "Home is where the heart is, we all know that. Still, and all, it doesn't do to underestimate what we might call The Adversary. She strikes me as being a highly capable young woman."

"Well," Daniel said comfortably, "I'm a highly capable old man."

"So you are, my dear man, so you are. And there's the fact that you're the boy's father: that's one up for you. All the same, we can't ignore the other fact: that she's his wife. And that gives *her* an advantage. The advantage of what we might call The Eternal Feminine. Not to be disgusting about it, Daniel, but only speaking medically, there's the simple matter of s-e-x."

"All right," Daniel said. "So there is. What about it?"

"What about s-e-x? A powerful weapon, my dear man. In the hands of an unscrupulous woman."

"Well, I have a few weapons of my own," Daniel said. "I didn't spend more than fifty years on stages all over the world without picking up a trick or two. And if I have to I'll use them all, and then we'll see what happens to your old friend s-e-x."

"Tooth and nail, Daniel?" Billy said. "Is that the order of the day?"

"It damn well is," Daniel said grimly. "Tooth and nail, and maybe a rabbit punch or two on the side. He'll come in here tonight, Billy, to put me out. But when he leaves, it'll be all settled, and settled my way. And I'll be here for good."

"Amazing, my dear man!" Billy said. "A triumph of the human spirit. And now, Daniel, we'd better make sure you're in shape for the great ordeal. We'd better have a little look at you!"

Abruptly he jumped from his chair and bustled across to Daniel's bed, where he began to fish impatiently through the large black satchel he had brought with him. It took him some time; he fumbled around, scattering small miscellaneous objects over the bedspread, whistling loudly all the while. Finally he found what he had been looking for. It was a blood pressure apparatus; triumphantly he snaked it out of the bag and held it up for Daniel to see.

"Here we are, my dear man," he said. "For a minute I thought I'd lost it or forgot, but it was all folded up underneath the can of dog food. Now just step over here, Daniel, if you will, and we'll see what's what!"

His voice was now brisk and authoritative, and Daniel obeyed at once, rolling up his right sleeve as he crossed the room. This was another of his little routines; it took place every week, and he enjoyed it thoroughly. He went through the examination without the slightest apprehension, for he was convinced of his own good health, and he had great faith in Billy. In general, he had always avoided doctors; on the few occasions he had visited them, the results had been unfortunate: they had charged him money, they had cured him no faster than he could have cured himself. And once, in Rome, he had had a positively frightening experience. He had had a boil near the base of his spine; it had persisted, interfering with his dancing; reluctantly, but on the recommendation of a fellow performer, he had consulted an Italian specialist. The specialist — a short, dead-white man in a morning coat, with hair like matted fur on the back of his hands — had listened to Daniel, had examined the boil, had announced the treatment. He would put a warm wire up Daniel's nose.

"Up my *nose!*" Daniel cried, years later, telling the story over and over to make his point. "The boil's on my arse and the wire's up my nose! How the hell do you like that for doctors?"

He had fled, of course, quickly and without paying, the visit having confirmed all his suspicions. He had not been to a doctor again, but from time to time he had heard stories of colleagues, less wise, who had gone for help with trifling complaints and had come back permanently maimed.

"Oh by God!" he had growled. "To hell with all those fellers!"

And so he had kept away from doctors until he had come back home and renewed his friendship with Billy. Billy, he felt, was different; there was no mystery, no nonsense, about Billy; he was miles ahead of the rest and, better still, had a contempt for them which rivaled Daniel's own. In most matters, he regarded himself as Billy's superior. They were good friends, but Daniel, for the most part, did the talking, and Billy did the listening. Daniel felt this was as it should be. In the one department of medicine, however, he held Billy in some awe.

Billy silently took his blood pressure now; afterwards, removing the strap, and stuffing the apparatus back into the satchel, he nodded and said, "As usual, Daniel, the pressure is perfect for a man of your years."

"I don't change much," Daniel said, with some complacence.

"You don't, my dear man. I can bear witness to

[53]

that. Medically speaking, you're the Rock of Gibraltar. Now we'll just make a note of that pressure: the systolic and the diastolic. Or, in the language of the layman, the upstairs and the downstairs." He looked through several pockets, apparently without success; he said, "Have you got a piece of paper, Daniel? Any old scrap will do."

"I've got an old envelope here somewhere, I think," Daniel said. Searching his own pockets, he finally produced a battered envelope, which he scrutinized carefully. "I don't know as you'd want this. It's got all grease spots on it. It's not the sort of thing you'd want to put a man's blood pressure on."

"It makes no difference, my dear man," Billy said, taking it. "None whatsoever. The man who knows his business doesn't need fancy leather record books. He has it all in his head. I've got the entire blueprint of your pressure, Daniel, right up here." He tapped his forehead with a finger; then, scribbling on the envelope, he stuffed it into a pants pocket. "And just to play it safe, it's also down here in the file." He patted the pants pocket loudly.

"By God, Billy," Daniel said, "I'm in a hell of a fix if you lose your memory or change your pants."

"Put your mind at ease, my dear man," Billy said. "Scientific precautions have been taken. I won't bother you with the nature of them, but they have. And next time I come in, I'll take the picture. Never forget the pictures, my dear man."

Daniel did not forget the pictures; he found them comforting. Once a month Billy came in and, after taking the pressure, stood him up against a wall and took his picture. The two men then compared that picture with pictures taken under similar circumstances during preceding months.

"What the pictures give us, Daniel," Billy said, "is photographic evidence. Proof positive that you're not decaying too fast."

"I'm damn well not decaying at all," Daniel said, slightly stung. "What the hell am I, a man or a tooth?"

"That's the personal approach you're taking, Daniel. That's not the scientific approach. Medical science uses no foam-rubber words. And you don't need them, my dear man. You're a miracle of constancy. But how would we know that if it wasn't for the pictures?"

"Oh, I'm all for the pictures, Billy. They're a great comfort to a man. Specially when they turn out right. And I'll tell you a funny thing about them: I never even heard of them till you came along."

"That's because I was the first to use them, my dear man," Billy said. "The whole technique was pioneered by me. I was the first man in the U.S.A. to bring the snapshot into the bedroom for medical purposes. That was four and a half years ago, Daniel, and I still say now exactly what I said then: 'The bedpan is important, yes, *but it can't do the work of the camera!'* "

"And I still say what I always said, Billy," Daniel said. "You'd of made a great doctor."

"Always remember, my dear man," Billy said, "that some of the very best men we have in medicine today don't go around calling themselves 'Doctor.' There are all different kinds of doctors. There are what we might call the Official Doctors that have gone through medical schools and have diplomas and all that nonsense. I have a very poor opinion of Official Doctors, Daniel."

"Yes, yes. I know. Still, they get most of the trade."

"The ignorant flocking to the ignorant, my dear man," Billy said. "Nothing more or less than that. It's the way of the world. You can't change that, Daniel."

[56]

"No, no, I suppose not." He spoke, now, a trifle abstractedly, and his eyes began to search restlessly around the room. He was beginning to weary of this subject, as old men sometimes do when the conversation works away from themselves. Besides, he had things to do. . . .

"But I wouldn't change it if I could," Billy said. "I'm far better off as it is, Daniel. I'm far better off not being an Official Doctor. I'm far better off being what you might call a Free Lancer of Medicine."

"You are, you are. And I'm far better off as I am." Daniel got to his feet, looking about him, establishing himself firmly in this place. "Right here. In this house. In this room. In a place I can call my home at last."

"Home sweet home, Daniel," Billy said, also rising, and picking up his satchel. "Contentment is everything. Well, my dear man. . . ."

He held out his hand; Daniel took it and said, "You'll be here this afternoon?"

"Wild horses couldn't keep me away, my dear man. I look forward to it with the highest anticipation!"

"There'll be no crowd," Daniel said. "Just you and Gottlieb and Father Feeley. But if you want to see how I'm going to handle them tonight, well, come around this afternoon and I'll show you the works."

"A preview of the battle plan!" Billy cried. "A private dress rehearsal of Waltzing Daniel Considine in action! My dear man, I'm honored and on tenterhooks! The question before the house is this: How are you going to do it? The technique employed: what's it to be? That's what we're all asking ourselves, my dear man!"

"Well, you'll damn well see for yourselves a couple of hours from now," Daniel said. He seated himself in his chair once more, reclining slightly, and closing his eyes. He raised one hand in a farewell salute and said abruptly, "Run along now, Billy. I've got to take my rest."

"The snooze before the battle!" Billy said admiringly. "Nerves of battleship steel! Just like the heavyweight champ! Goodbye, my dear man! I'll be back at the appointed hour, never fear!"

He opened the door and let himself out quickly; Daniel was alone. He was grateful for this. He liked Billy, Billy was a good friend, none better, thought Daniel, but all the same, he could tire a man out with all that chat. All about himself, too. . . .

He had opened his eyes to make sure that Billy was gone. Now he closed them again, but he did not sleep. Instead, he began to go over his plans, very carefully, still once more. He was confident, but he did not want to make even the slightest mistake. Too much depended on it. . . .

three

THE law office for which Tom worked was the oldest in the city. It had a first-family clientele, tea was served daily at four, and old Mr. Pomeroy, the senior partner of the firm, had a rolltop desk in his office, ate sourballs, and personally conducted the really important trial work with a style which was the envy of all who aspired to well-bred brutality. It was always understood, although never explicitly stated, that there were certain types of cases which the firm did not handle; after working here for twenty years, Tom found it hard to imagine just what those cases might be.

He was pleasantly and even rather profitably employed. He was not a major figure in the office, but neither was he unimportant. Like many similar firms, this one periodically refreshed itself with a number of bright young men. A few of these did very well; some did well enough; the rest, after a suitable period, were politely diverted to shabbier or shinier firms, or to the government. Tom, a bright young man of twenty years ago, had done well enough.

This morning he worked steadily, not because what he had to do was urgent, but because he had decided that in this way he could at least distract himself from the problem of his father. He was wrong; he had been working less than an hour when the telephone rang.

"Mr. Considine? Hello there: this is Brother Martin? At Saint Vincent's Smiling Valley?"

Tom's wife had done most of the spadework at the Smiling Valley; he had gone there only once. Still, he remembered the brother — not young, not old, but bouncy, jubilant, talkative — who had greeted them, who had led them around, who had not left their side. This had been Brother Martin: smiling, heavy-faced, with little ringlets of hair the color of dust and a fighter's nose. He said, "Yes, good morning, Brother."

"Isn't it one of the best!" Brother Martin said enthusiastically. "I'll tell you why I called, Mr. Considine. I called to firm up arrangements. We can expect Dad sometime this evening or tomorrow?"

Tom remembered that it was towards the end

of his single visit to the Smiling Valley that his father had become "Dad" to Brother Martin. He had felt vaguely uncomfortable at the time; he felt the same now. Was this institutional cosiness? Or was it Brother Martin? He said, "Yes, I'm not sure about the time just yet. I'd imagine it would be somewhere around the middle of the morning."

"We'll expect you when we see you, then," Brother Martin said, and laughed. Somewhat disconcertingly he added, "Good-oh!"

To himself Tom said quickly: *Over and out.* Into the telephone he said, "If there should be any changes in the time, Brother, we'll let you know. And thanks very much for your call."

He prepared to hang up, but Brother Martin had not finished. "Oh, by the bye," he said. "Good news about three-oh-four!"

"Three-oh-four?"

"The room Mrs. Considine was so wild about. Third floor, southwest corner? We both thought it would be just about ideal for Dad, but unfortunately at the time we spoke it was occupied."

"And now it's not?"

"No," said Brother Martin. "No, not any more."

There was a silence; Tom thought: *Enough said.* Which was all right with him, certainly; he said briskly, "Well, again, thanks for your call, Brother. And we'll see you tomorrow."

"Poor Mrs. Cass!" Brother Martin said, with sudden emotion. "Old age, of course, plus all the complications. Oh my, we get an awful lot of that out here. Well, naturally. Being what we are. But wouldn't you think we'd get used to it? My trouble is, I can't. What I mean is, I get too deeply involved. I suppose it's my own fault. Some of the others are much more matter-of-fact. Brother Harold, for instance. He's a great one for telling me not to get so upset. And when poor Mrs. Cass died on Thursday, all he said was that it came as no surprise to him! Well, for crying out loud, it came as no surprise to *me,* either! What does he think I am, some kind of rookie, or something? *I* knew," Brother Martin said, somewhat inelegantly, "she was going to cash in her chips! I've been around here a very long time. I know all the ropes, believe you me! But still, that doesn't prevent me from having feelings, does it?"

Brother Martin was indignant; he seemed to be panting. Tom said, "Look, Brother —"

"But," Brother Martin said, recovering his good spirits with astonishing speed, "that's the way the ball bounces. And what a dull old world it would

be if everybody was like everybody else! So poor
Mrs. Cass is gone. With her funny little face and
her funny little smile and her funny little songs.
I'll miss her, Mr. Considine. Oh, I miss them all,
of course, but some I miss more than others.
That's only human, isn't it? And Mrs. Cass was
always such a help to me. The burdens she lifted
from my shoulders with her cheering little ways!
Oh, I can tell you, that means so much in a community such as ours!"

And Tom, who had no wish to extend this conversation, nevertheless suddenly felt it was important that he ask this absurd man a question. He
said, "The old, Brother: you deal with them day
after day. Is it as difficult as it seems to be?"

"Oh," Brother Martin said doubtfully, "I don't
know about that. It's not easy, of course. The old
have their special problems, you know. They get
sick quite often and quite easily, and in the most
alarming ways. At least they alarm me. And they
do have this feeling that nobody much wants them;
I suppose that makes them disagreeable now and
then. And then if you do something for them
they're not always terribly grateful. But," he said
cheerily, "they're not so bad, really. And somebody's got to take care of them, haven't they? So

I tease them and jolly them along, and we have our good times together. And sometimes they pitch in and help out. That's where poor Mrs. Cass was a real peach. Always playing the piano or singing or cheering them up. A born clown. Believe you me, when someone like that goes, it leaves a gap, Mr. Considine. A gap that's very very hard to fill. I think that's probably why I'm really so excited about your father's arrival."

This was a new note; Tom said carefully, "I wouldn't count on my father to fill any gaps of that kind, Brother. Don't be misled by the fact that he was an entertainer —"

"And what an entertainer!" Brother Martin said. "Oh my, if I could only tell you the number of times I've seen him in person! On the stage of Fay's Theater, in Providence, Rhode Island. That's where I grew up, Mr. Considine. In good old Little Rhody. Actually, this may surprise you, but I didn't leave Providence until I was nearly twenty-seven."

Oh God, thought Tom. He said patiently, "But that was long ago, Brother. My point is that my father isn't a very gregarious man at the present time. I think he'd appreciate it most if he were simply let alone. . . ."

"I'm older than I look, you see," explained

Brother Martin. "I had what's usually termed a delayed vocation, so naturally when I came into the Order I was somewhat older than the other fellows. Oh, for the longest time there, I didn't know what I wanted to be. Once upon a time I thought I'd like to write: short stories, you know, and novels. And then I had this feeling that maybe I should go on the stage. Quite a few nice people said I had all kinds of promise. But then along came my vocation and that was the end of that. I wound up here doing God's work and all!"

It seemed to Tom that nearly everyone he had met or talked to in connection with his father had been very close to certifiable. He started to speak, then stopped. He knew that whatever he said, it would not be heard.

"Yes," Brother Martin was saying, "here I came, and here I stayed. Golly, when you think of the *man-hours* I've checked off in this pad! But that's what having a vocation means, doesn't it? And I've never regretted a minute, actually. It's been so interesting. And the people I've been lucky enough to meet! People I never could have met on the outside. People like . . . well, like *Dad*. Did you know that Dad was my boyhood idol, Mr. Considine? He was. He brought a little bit of happiness to a boy who needed happiness badly. Believe you me, there was darned little magic in *my* young life. You see, I was the product of a broken home. The theater was my refuge. Fay's Theater. I used to go there day after day. . . ."

He talked on and Tom ceased to listen. Some minutes later the monologue ended: just how, Tom did not know. There seemed to be some sort of interruption at the other end. He thought he heard shouts, there was a strange noise like static, and with a goodbye so hurried it was garbled Brother Martin was gone. Tom hung up slowly. It had not been a reassuring talk; moreover, it had raised certain doubts. . . .

In the house, Daniel was also on the telephone; like his son, he now listened rather than talked. His sister Delia had called him; she had been talking for some time, and he listened to the high powerful whine with resignation and resentment. It was his only sister, and yet, why should he have someone like this as his only sister? He was an old man, it was unfair. . . .

". . . but no information as well," she was complaining. "If some of my friends ask me about you, what can I tell them? I'll tell you what I can tell them: *nothing*. You're back a full year now and I still don't know any more than the day you came."

Daniel said, "You were always a very inquisitive woman, Delia."

"Inquisitive! I swear to God, you go away, you stay away for twenty years with only a cheap postcard now and then, and all of a sudden you come back one night out of the blue without so much as a word of warning, and when the only sister you've got in the world asks you where you were and how you were and what you did, all you say is, 'I was dancing!'"

It was ground covered many times before; Daniel said wearily, "Well, what's so strange about that? That's what I did. I'm a dancer — so I danced. I danced everywhere, all over the world. I danced in palaces and jungles. So that's where I was, and that's what I did. And as for my health it was fine all the time. I've told you that a thousand times since I got back. What more do you want to know?"

"I want *normal* information, that's what I want," Delia said. "The same as anybody else would want. And the same as anybody else would give. Coming back to us all as if you'd left only five minutes before, when the last time I saw you you were doing your silly dance in Loew's State Theater, and that was twenty years ago!"

"That's another thing I remember about you, Delia," Daniel said. "You never got anything straight. It wasn't Loew's State you saw me play; it was the Poli-Palace. And it wasn't twenty years ago; it was twenty-one."

"You've got a marvelous memory, haven't you, Daniel?" Delia said scornfully. "You can remember that the head usher at King Big Ben's Theater in London, England, had a walleye and a wart on the side of his nose, but when it comes to your own family we're lucky you even remember our names!"

"Twenty-one years ago," Daniel said broodingly. "By God, I won't forget that in a hurry. It was the week they bombed Pearl Harbor, and who did I have on the bill with me but a couple of Jap jugglers. Japs, at a time like that! The Asaka Brothers, their names were. The crowd threw everything but the seats at them. After the first show I grabbed one of them and I said, 'For the love of God, Asaka, get out of here now or else change your name in a hurry. Make believe you're Chinamen; call yourselves the Hong Kong Mystery Boys or anything you want, but do it before the next show or you'll all be murdered. And I'll be damned if I'm going to do my dance on a stage full of dead Japs!' Well, they changed the name, but it did no good. Oh, I tell you, it was one hell of a week for me. As long as I live, I'll never forget Pearl Harbor!"

"That's fine, Daniel!" Delia cried. "Oh, that's fine! That's just what I called to hear! A lot of rubbishy nonsense about Jap acrobats that nobody knows and nobody cares about! When what I want to know is about you and what you did *besides* dance. You had to live: what kind of a house did you live in? Who did you meet? Were you ever in jail? Did you get married again after Rose died? I wouldn't put it past you!"

"I didn't get married, Delia," Daniel said, "but I did the next best thing. I took up with a colored woman in Zanzibar and raised a family of twelve. They're all the spittin' image of you, Delia. Chocolate-colored, you know, but you all the same. And I was in jail only once, the time they gave me ten years for exposing myself in public helicopters. Good God Almighty, stop asking silly questions!"

"I'm sorry if my questions don't suit you, Daniel, but then I haven't had much practice, have I? You never spent that much time with us. Specially with your poor wife. If you ever came home at all it was for a square meal, and then you were off on the morning train with your dancing pumps in your pocket. Dancing Daniel Considine!"

"*Waltzing* Daniel Considine," Daniel said sharply, for it was a mistake he had corrected before. "Not *Dancing*. *Waltzing*. That was always my billing. I was always called Waltzing Daniel Considine."

"Well, whatever you were called," Delia said. "I could never see what all the fuss was about anyways. A full-grown man making his living out of dancing. And a lot of people silly enough to pay good money to see you."

"They'll never be able to say that about you, Delia. You always came in on a pass. All the same, you always came, didn't you?"

"I had no choice!" Delia said. "I had my loyalty to the family, even if you didn't. When all my friends said to me, 'Well, Delia, I suppose you'll be down in the front row tonight, cheering your brother along,' I couldn't very well tell them I'd rather be anywheres else. Doing something sensible. No, I was always too loyal for that. So I always went to see you, *and I was always ashamed.* All those people yelling and laughing their heads off the minute you put your foot on the stage! How do you think I felt at that?"

"You should of felt damn good," Daniel said

wearily. "Good God Almighty, they were supposed to laugh! That was the idea of the whole thing: how many times do you have to be told? It was a comedy dance act. It was the best damn comedy dance act in the business. Anybody that had any sense of fun at all knew that!"

"Well, here's one that didn't, and I have a grand sense of fun. I'd hate to tell you how many people come up to me on the street and say, 'I wish I had your sense of fun, Delia.' But I never saw anything to laugh at in my own brother running out onto a stage and making a fool of himself, dancing around without even a live woman for a partner, but an old floor mop dressed up to look like one!"

Daniel said, "There's some people should never be let near a theater, Delia, and you're one of them. I know your grand sense of fun. Your idea of a good time is to have your supper and then run around to Saint Benedict's and kneel down with half a dozen like yourself and say the rosary out loud. That way you can keep talking all night long. Hail Mary cluck cluck cluck!"

"That's right, Daniel!" she cried. "Oh, that's right: be blasphemous! That shows you're a man of the world. That shows you've traveled. And that shows why the only priest that's willing to come near you is somebody like Father Frank Feeley!"

"He's damn well the only one I let near me," Daniel said. "And what's supposed to be wrong with him?"

"He's all right, I guess," Delia said. She added virtuously, "It's not up to me to judge. All the same, if I wanted a priest I don't know that I'd pick one that's been seen at every racetrack from Canada to Mexico."

"All right, he used to go to the races. He liked horses; it was his hobby. Is that a sin?"

"They say he always wanted to be a jockey," Delia said, "only he was too tall."

Daniel's visual imagination was not his greatest strength, but without any trouble at all he could see his sister as she sat by the telephone: small, beaky, and seething, all in black — black dress, black cotton stockings, a great black cabbage of a hat. This was the only picture he could summon up of his sister these days; even when he tried to think of her as a little girl, he could see only the aged fury in her mourning clothes. And mourning for *what*? Dave? The man had died thirty years ago, and hadn't been much to begin with. Daniel had always held the poorest opinion of Delia's husband: a thick-faced man with too many teeth who had been the oldest altar boy in the history of the diocese and who had died, in fact, of a child's disease. . . .

He said now, "It's a damn lucky thing you and Dave never had a child. It would of turned out to be a parrot."

"Never mind about me and Dave," Delia said sharply. "At least when Dave was alive I had a marvelous husband that was always by my side, and we both know women in this city that couldn't say the same, don't we, Daniel? Oh yes we do!"

"You know, Delia," Daniel said, "over the years people would come up to me sometimes and ask me what sort of a place I came from, what my home town was like. Do you know what I always told them? I always told them it was the only town in the world where all the women had tongues that went like a woodpecker's beak, all day long. Or maybe I wasn't fair. Maybe not all the women were like that. Maybe only two of them were. The one I married. And the one I got for a sister."

"I'm surprised you mentioned us at all," Delia said. "The town, your wife, *or* me. I didn't think you knew any of us that well. They say you have to spend a little time with someone to get to know them. Oh, yes. . . ."

[74]

She went on talking and Daniel, putting the re-
ceiver down, went out to the bathroom. When he
came back she was still talking and so, cutting in,
he said abruptly, "All right, Delia. That'll do now.
Thanks for the call. I've got to go."

"The same old gracious Daniel," she said, "with
the same lovely manners he always had. Never
mind, I hope I'm big enough to ignore them. And
I'll be in to see you late in the day all the same."

"No," he said. "Don't come in. I'm busy today.
I've got a lot of things to do."

"Oh that's right!" Delia said, in her crowing
voice. "That's right: today is moving day. I almost
forgot, Daniel. This is the last day in the nice soft
nest. Tomorrow you'll be out here to the Valley.
Oh my, aren't we the lucky people! Oh yes! I wonder will they have a band to meet you? I wonder —"

Daniel hung up. He did not hang up in anger or
in sudden exasperation; he had simply felt like
hanging up, and so he had. It was the way he finished all telephone conversations with his sister:
at some point he got tired and hung up. The visits
were harder to handle. Since he had come home
these visits had been frequent and regular; he had
not enjoyed them. And yet he had admitted her;

he had wasted his time talking to her; he had never thrown her out. But kindness, he felt, could be pushed too far. . . .

"Watch out!" he cried aloud. "All silly bitches that keep after a patient man, watch out!"

He knew that in spite of what he had said, she would come to see him that afternoon. Today of all days, wild horses couldn't keep her away. He knew the type, they were all alike. *In at the kill,* he thought, *jaws dripping with spit: that's the place they want to be!*

But he had a surprise for them.

"Bad news!" he cried now, staring at himself in the mirror. "Oh, terrible news! There'll be no kill today!"

And, still in front of the mirror, he began to practice the finishing touches, the little details of his scheme which, eventually, could make all the difference.

Shortly before lunch, Tom had another telephone call and this time, to his relief, it was not an interruption. It was his wife.

He greeted her and said immediately, "Any news?"

"No, it's just so cuckoo you can't imagine it," she

said. "I don't know what's going to happen. He's
crazy. Really crazy, I think. And Anna's not much
better. And the worst of it is that it all looks so
normal. You know: they both play golf and they
both play bridge and they have a nice house with a
flagstone patio and a barbecue pit and a Volks-
wagen and a station wagon and two kids. The kids
are great, but Anna and Simon are right out of the
Marx Brothers. Except it really isn't very funny.
Golly," she sighed, "will I be glad to get home!"

A week ago she had gone to visit her sister; she
had gone reluctantly. She and her sister were
friendly without being close; the two almost never
saw each other, and within any given year there
might be an exchange of a postcard or two, nothing more. Suddenly, however, letters had begun to
come from Anna, now located in Detroit with her
mysterious husband. (Mysterious in that neither
Tom nor Ellen had ever met him or knew anything
about him save his name: Simon Collingwood.)
These letters had contained hints that a visit from
Ellen would be welcome; in the last letter the hints
had broadened into frank appeal. And finally Ellen
had agreed to go. Packing, she had said to Tom,
"Although what's the point? I'm no good at this. I
don't know him at all, and I don't even know Anna

[77]

very well these days. So what can I do? Except listen. I guess maybe that's what she wants."

So she had gone. Unwillingly, but not altogether so; in one obvious sense the timing of the trip was providential. At the airport she had said, "I'll be back a week from today. In the afternoon. Anyway, there's only the one flight. So I'll see you then." She had kissed him, then stood back and looked at him, warning and some doubt in the large gray eyes. "*Just* you: right?" she had said.

He had promised again. "Just me."

"Honest to Pete?"

"Honest to Pete."

Had she believed this? Not entirely, he knew, but enough so that she had exhaled in relief, grabbed him, held him tight, kissed him once more, hard, and then had gone.

And now she was coming back. He listened without interest as she talked a bit more about the domestic troubles of two people he did not know. His mind was here, on a problem of greater concern, and so, evidently, was hers, for unexpectedly she broke off her description of her sister's most recent difficulties and said, "Have they called yet? From Saint Vincent's?"

"Yes, just a while ago." Briefly, he told her of his

conversation with Brother Martin. He said, "Who is he, anyway? I don't quite get him in all this."

"Brother Martin? Oh," she said indulgently, "he's all right."

"No," he said firmly, "he's not that. I don't know what else he is, but he's certainly not all right."

"Well, I mean, he's harmless," she said. "He has no *authority*. He puts on a great show, walking around and talking to people and making these telephone calls, but he doesn't actually *do* anything. As far as running the place goes."

"Are there any more like that out there?"

"Like Brother Martin?" She sounded puzzled. "No, not that I know of. Why would there be? He's an oddball, but the rest of them all seem to be competent, experienced . . . hey!" she said, her tone suddenly different. "What's up?"

He said, "Look, about this harmless Brother Martin: I'd say he was just about ready to fall off his rocker. If he's not off already. The point is that if that place has a few more Brother Martins running around loose, then we could be letting ourselves in for some trouble."

He did not really anticipate trouble; in his brief tour of the Smiling Valley he had seen nothing to support apprehension. He had only this absurd telephone conversation, which probably meant nothing. Yet it had left him peculiarly unsettled; later in the afternoon, sitting at his desk and thinking about it, he had even had a picture of his father, wandering in lonely wariness around the unfamiliar grounds of the institution, and being taken by surprise by a circling ring of men, all of whom resembled Brother Martin. Brown-robed, roguish but burly, they had come out of nowhere to surround the old man, closing in on him, laughing, tugging at him, urgently demanding a sample of the old soft shoe, *pro bono publico.* . . .

He realized that this vision was not quite rational. He had been angry with himself for entertaining it at the time; he was slightly ashamed of himself for recalling it now. He said quickly, "It's only that I don't want him harassed."

"Who'll harass him?" she asked. "Brother Martin? He won't even have to see Brother Martin if he doesn't want to. He won't have to see anybody; he can be absolutely by himself if he likes. Or he can have whatever visitors he wants, whenever he wants them. It's not a prison; it's a perfectly good place where they understand old people. So he won't be harassed at all. And anyway, I thought that was the whole point of sending him there: so that nobody would be harassed any more. Your father *or* us."

She was logical, patient, fair; from this he knew that she was both exasperated and apprehensive. Reassuringly he said, "It's okay; I know. I was just checking out the possibilities. And don't worry: I'm not having second thoughts or making last-minute switches. It's all set. Just the way we said."

"Is it? Well, that's good, because it's pretty awful out here, but I'd even stay here for a while rather than come back if he were still . . . Tommy, it'd be just *ghastly!*" The apprehension had come through; anxiously, almost pleadingly, she said, "Wouldn't it?"

He agreed that it would be ghastly. He had known for months how she had felt about his father — he could hardly not have known — but it was not until one night, nearly five weeks ago, that she had declared herself explicitly in a night-long, occasionally hysterical bill of complaints. They had been in bed; suddenly he had felt her trembling, and heard her weeping softly. Surprised — for this had not happened before — and concerned, he had asked what was wrong, and had been answered with more weeping. Alarmed, he had pressed harder, and finally it had come out.

It had come pouring out, and as he should have known from the first, it was Daniel. Not any one thing about Daniel, and certainly nothing new that he had done that day. It was just Daniel: the continuing, cumulative, ever-present fact of Daniel. . . .

"It's just not my house any more," she had sobbed. "It just *isn't* . . . every day, day after day . . . he's everywhere . . . he's got that soft walk, I can't even hear him coming . . . that awful old man: I'm sorry, I know he's your father and all that, but that's what he is . . . and all those friends I don't know and don't ever want to know . . . in my house . . . I can't even make a phone call or even go to the *bathroom* in privacy any more . . . he's just eating us up . . . and it's so crazy *because you don't even like him.* . . ."

This had gone on for a long time, with Tom consoling her, promising over and over again that he would take steps at last, that he would be firm; towards morning she had gone to sleep. But Tom had stayed awake, reproaching himself: he should have done something about his father long ago. For everything — *everything* — she had said was true; everything she had felt he had felt himself — yet he had done nothing. Out of inertia, partly;

[82]

he knew it was his fault to be easygoing in most matters; he preferred solutions that came without his direct intervention. And too, with his father, no matter what his feeling towards him, he was for some reason unwilling to move. . . .

But now of course he had to. He had not known that his wife had felt so strongly, so *violently* — she had in fact done a complete turnabout on his father. For when he had arrived, and for the first few days — perhaps even weeks — she had been interested in, and charmed by, the old man. She had found him picturesque; she had listened, fascinated, to the stories of his travels and his triumphs. Too young for vaudeville herself, she had been enchanted by this representative of a world she had never seen and of which she had just barely heard. She had previously known Daniel only through her husband's rare mentions of him, and these had not been sympathetic; in these early days she sometimes charged Tom with having been unfair in the matter of his father.

"I suppose he must have been terrible, in a way," she had said, "going off like that. But you wouldn't know it now, would you? I think he's an old sweetie!"

But the old sweetie's charm had not endured.

Slowly, at first, then more rapidly, it had worn away, not because there had been any change in Daniel, but precisely because there had been no change in him. Picturesqueness withered before familiarity; Ellen came soon enough to see that the entertaining transient was in fact a self-centered and determined old man who had decided to make what was hers his own. It was as simple as that. The discovery had appalled her; she had grown cooler towards Daniel, he had disregarded her; then, finally, after many hints and fragments of discussion, there had come the emotional all-night session with Tom. It was after that that the two of them had notified Daniel of their decision; since that time he had been in upstairs isolation; she had found this to be, if anything, slightly more unbearable than his earlier unpredictable wandering.

So that he had to go: Tom knew this. Indeed, now that the date had been set, he literally could not imagine his father's continuing with them a week, even a day, longer. He told this to Ellen now over the telephone; he said, "And so I'll see him tonight, right after dinner. We'll have the one last talk, and that'll be that."

She said, "What time are you seeing him?"

"Seven. Eight. It doesn't matter much, does it?

Except that the sooner the better, I guess," he said. "I don't suppose it'll be any too pleasant, and I'd just as soon get it over with."

"What are you going to say to him? I mean, in case he starts . . . well, kicking up a fuss? I know he said he'd go and all that, but I don't believe him for a minute. Do you?"

"No. Not very much. And I don't know exactly what I'm going to say, either. I don't think you can blueprint a thing like this; I think you more or less have to play it by ear. Which is what I'm going to do. I'll let him talk and say what he has to say. And he can't kick up too much of a fuss, honey, for one simple reason: *we've got all the cards.* He can't change that."

"I know," she said. But she sounded just a bit doubtful; then, with a sudden urgency, she said, "Look, love: be very careful, will you? He's really *so* tricky. And he'll pull out all the stops tonight, you know he will! So whatever he pulls, don't let him get away with it, will you? Do you promise?"

He promised. He knew that Ellen was almost neurotically respectful of the old man's cunning, and that no matter what he said to her, she would not really be convinced that Daniel was going until in fact he had gone. In a sense, Tom felt, this was

[85]

not entirely flattering to him; nevertheless, he understood it, and he loved his young wife. So he talked now, once more in terms of reassurance, promising her still again that when she returned tomorrow she would return to her own home, with her husband there, and with — at last — the guest room vacant.

When he finished, and they had both hung up, he felt sure that she believed him. In a way. . . .

four

WHEN, that afternoon, Delia came to visit him, as she promised she would, and as Daniel knew she would, he had determined, at first, not to let her in. But she had stood outside his bedroom door, shouting through it in her high invariable voice, and in the interest of his own peace, and because he thought he might really get rid of her faster that way, he had opened the door grudgingly and she had burst in, talking. Now she was still talking, and Daniel talked too. He knew this was wrong; experience had taught him that the nonstop talker was uncomfortable and eventually stilled in the face of total silence. In spite of this, she drew him in. Angered, exasperated, or merely impatient, he responded, and that was all she needed. . . .

". . . some people that travel come home once in a blue moon, just to show they know where their house is. And some people that travel write letters every year or so, just to tell their own family how they are. But who knew whether you were dead or alive? Who knew?"

"I did," Daniel said.

"Yes, you did. And what about Tom? Your own son. Did he know you right away the night you came back? Or was there a bit of confusion on the doorstep? Did he say to you, 'Go away now: we don't want any brushes today?' And did you laugh and say to him, 'I have a little surprise for you, Tom. I'm not the Fuller Brush Man; I'm your famous Dad'?"

"By God," Daniel said, "I'd almost forgot how cosy these talks with you could be, Delia. It's like being in a phone booth with a puff adder. Of course the boy knew me. Why wouldn't he? I'm his father."

"His father that he hadn't seen for twenty years," Delia said. "And the wife: she'd never seen you at all, had she? Well well well. They must of been tickled pink, the two of them. Specially the wife. I'll bet she's almost out of her mind with happiness when all your friends come round to call. She's met them all by now, I suppose."

Daniel said only, "She's met some, not all."

"Well, the more the merrier. I imagine that's what she must say to herself every time she's busy with the housework and the phone rings or there's a knock on the door and she answers it and it's for you. Has she met Billy Ryan, the well-known fake doctor, yet? There's a lovely addition to a living room. Or old Gottlieb, that Jewish feller that nobody ever knew what he did except go to the theater to see you?"

Daniel tried another tack. "You mustn't be jealous, Delia. Not everybody in a family can be popular. There's always the ugly duckling. And I wouldn't be surprised if every once in a while someone didn't come out to the Smiling Valley to see you. Some little nun, maybe, that wanted someone that wasn't too bright to crochet holy mottoes onto flour bags."

But today, for some reason, it did not work; he was disappointed. She said only, "Sarcasm never bothered me, Daniel. I was always above it. And you'll have a chance to see for yourself about my visitors, won't you? From now on? And let me tell you another thing: *you're very lucky to get into the Smiling Valley.* Oh, there's other places, of course, but it's the Smiling Valley that everybody wants to get into. On account of the lovely facilities."

[89]

"I don't give a damn about the lovely facilities," Daniel said. "If they had two toilets and a television in every room I still wouldn't go there."

Curiously, this stung where the other had not; Delia said sharply, "Oh, you wouldn't? It's not good enough for you, I suppose? It's good enough for Mrs. Arthur B. Maguire, the widow of the late cocoa king, but it's not good enough for you!"

"What the hell has she got to do with it?" Daniel said. He looked at his watch; he had not time for much more of this. "All I'm telling you is this, for the hundredth time: good enough or bad enough, it makes no difference. I'm not going to the Smiling Valley. I'm not going anywhere. I'm staying. Right here."

Delia, suddenly businesslike, said, "Now, Daniel, that's enough of that. Fun is fun, no one knows that better than I do, but you're not in Loew's State Theater now. You're in real life and you've got to face facts. And the first fact is you're not going to stay in this house. Oh, you may want to, I don't doubt that: you always had an eye for the soft berth. But you're going to be swept right out of this one, and you know why. Because she won't have you."

"You're an expert on that too, are you, Delia?"

he said. "You know just what she thinks and just what she wants, is that it?"

"I don't say that," Delia said. "All I know is what she doesn't want, and what she doesn't want above all else is a lifetime boarder by the name of Dancing Daniel Considine."

"*Waltzing* Daniel Considine!" Daniel said angrily. "What the hell is wrong with you? How many times do you have to be told?"

"Waltzing, fox-trotting, or deep-knee-bending, she still doesn't want you. And I can't say as I blame her. She doesn't even know you. She doesn't want to know you. And why should she? Tom is the man she married and Tom is the man she wants to live with. Not Tom's Dad that didn't even come to his own son's wedding."

"How could I of come to the wedding?" Daniel said. "I wasn't even told there was a wedding till two weeks after it happened!"

"And why was that?" Delia cried. "Why was that, Daniel? I'll tell you why: it was because nobody in your own family knew where you were to send word to you. And suppose you were told, would you of come? Oh no, Daniel. Not you. Your own son's wedding is all very well, but it's not in the same

[91]

class as playing Waltz-Me-Around-Again-Willie five times a day on a stage in Venezuela!"

"Now I'll tell *you* something," Daniel said triumphantly. "*I never played Venezuela in my life.* Nor anywhere else in South America. I remember one time they tried to book me down there with Orville Stamm the Strong Boy and Thelma De Onzo the World's Greatest Candlestick Jumper. But I wouldn't go. I said to them, 'If you think I'm going to do my dance in front of a crowd of hopped-up Indians all waiting to get at my head to shrink it down to the size of a golf ball, you've got another think coming. No no,' I said, 'you don't know Waltzing Daniel Considine. Go get yourself another boy: I wouldn't go down there for a million dollars.' And I didn't. I played almost all over the world, but I never played South America!"

"Is that a fact, Daniel?" she said. "Is that a fact?" With some detachment Daniel watched the little lined bird's face as it grew gleefully sharper; *There's a really homely woman,* he thought. "Well, that's a great blow to me!" she said. "I was positive a world traveler like yourself had been everywhere and done everything. Not like the rest of us poor stay-at-homes that just minded our business and lived up to our obligations. But that's no matter

now. All I'm saying to you is that this girl has her
own life to live — hers and Tom's. And you can
bet your boots she's not going to keep on living it
in a house where she has to be a part-time usher
for fake doctors, mysterious Jews, and priests that
might just as well be jockeys. 'Come right in, go
right up the stairs, and first turn to the left to see
His Lordship Daniel Considine!' Oh no, Daniel.
Not this girl. That's not her style at all!"

"I don't know what her style is, and what's more
I don't care," Daniel said. "Who gives a damn what
she will or she won't do? She hasn't the say; it's not
her house. It's Tom's house, and if you have to be
reminded again, Tom's my son."

"I don't have to be reminded," Delia said, "although I don't know that I can say the same for
Tom. He's been your son for more than forty years,
and the only times he saw you was between trains!"

She was a tiring woman. He closed his eyes,
then opened them, and said with finality, "All
right: I wasn't home much. I could of stayed home
more. I could of stayed home like the rest of the
coast defenders and spent my life dancing my feet
off for trolley car fare. I could of stayed home and
been like you and come to the end of my days going nowhere and seeing nothing but the city hall

roof and the back of the next man's neck. I could of stayed home and fought like hell with Rose every day. But I didn't. I went away. And as far as Tom goes, I might not of seen him much, but I supported him damn well. He went to the best schools money could buy, and he went to them all the way. All right, so I wasn't at hand every blessed minute, but what I made was. And don't ever forget this: what he's got today he owes to one man. Me!"

"And now," Delia said, "you've decided to give him a little bit more. You've decided to give him yourself: Daniel Considine, His Dad in Person. And is Tom supposed to do handsprings and say to the wife, 'Make way for my invisible Dad, that's come back to me at last — I'm his Sonny Boy and he's the one that counts with me'? Don't talk foolish, Daniel. Use the brains God gave you and start packing your bags. She doesn't want you, and neither does he. The young don't want old people around: haven't you even learned that yet? We're too slow for them, we mix up their lives, we get in the way. That goes double for someone like you, someone that they hardly even know. So pack up, Daniel, because you've got till tonight. Then out you go!"

"You're sure of that, are you, Delia?" he said. "Well, then, I guess it must be so, if a smart woman like you says it is."

"Oh, I know you've got a trick up your sleeve," she said. "I heard all about you being mild as milk and telling them, 'Yes, yes, I'll go if that's what you want. Just make my reservations and tell me the day.' That may fool some people, but I know it's all a lie. I know you've got one of your little schemes you think will make them take it all back and keep you here. Well, I'll tell you this much, Daniel: whatever it is, it won't work. Not this time. Not with them. Mark my words, Daniel, you're all done. Come tonight and out you go!"

"A talk with you is like a month in the country, Delia," Daniel said. "I'll tell you what: if you can get out of the lockup, why don't you come around tonight and see for yourself? Come around and bring your friends. All those old maid chums of yours. Specially that cockeyed one that used to see the Blessed Virgin in the fireplace every night. I imagine they'd be tickled to death to come. 'Come along, girls,' you could say. 'Come along and watch my brother Daniel get kicked out on his arse!'"

"The same old dirty tongue, I see, Daniel," Delia said. "Some people never lose it. And some people never have it. Well, no matter now. I'll see what I can do for you at the Smiling Valley. I'll try to get you a room in the new wing. I might even get you down next to Mrs. Arthur B. Maguire. Although I don't promise a thing. I —"

She was interrupted by a sharp knock on the door. It was the code knock; it was both expected and welcome. Daniel, with a plain gesture of relief, hurried to the door and opened it. A priest stood in the hall: a small dapper man of approximately Daniel's age with neat gray hair and a thin nervous face. He stepped quickly into the room without speaking, nodding at Daniel, and stopping abruptly when he saw Delia.

"Family conference?" he said. "I'll be back."

"No no," Daniel said hurriedly. "Come in, come in. You know my sister, Delia Bresnahan?"

The priest said, "Everyone knows Mrs. Bresnahan."

"Good afternoon, Father," Delia said stiffly.

"If I'd known you were to be here this afternoon, Mrs. Bresnahan," the priest said, looking at her with great directness, "I'd have worn my jockey hat."

Delia shot a venomous glance at Daniel; when she spoke it was with less than her customary assurance. "I . . . well, I see you like a little joke, Father."

"I'm full of fun," the priest said grimly.

"Yes yes, that's a matter of common knowledge," Delia said, very rapidly. "I often say to my friends, I say, 'I wish all priests could take a little joke like Father Frank Feeley!' "

This met silence: a forbidding silence. Delia looked first at the priest, then at Daniel; both said nothing. Finally Delia said uncomfortably, "Well, what I meant to say was, I guess my business here is done. I wouldn't want to keep you from your talk."

"Goodbye, Delia," Daniel said.

"Goodbye, goodbye, Daniel," she said, almost gratefully. "I'll be in again one day soon, same as always. Well, I won't be in here exactly, things being what they are, but wherever you are, I'll . . . well, goodbye, Father."

This met more silence and the briefest of nods; smiling and bobbing nervously, Delia backed her way out of the room in haste.

Father Feeley, watching her leave, said, "There goes a terrible human being."

"One of the worst," Daniel said agreeably.

"Simply to be exposed to something like that on

a daily basis would shrivel a man to a crisp," Father Feeley said. "Yet she was married. I always say a prayer for the husbands of women like that."

Daniel said, "I read stories now and again where a man gets old and he's sitting in a chair and all of a sudden he takes a good look at somebody else in his family that's got old too, and he says to himself, 'My my! What in the world happened to make poor Sally turn out like that? Where's the gay little girl I used to know?' Well, I never say anything like that about Delia, because I know what happened: *nothing* happened. She was always the way she is now. Even as a child she was about as gay as a panther."

"One of a type," Father Feeley said. "Sooner or later they all turn to religion. That's what's really terrifying. The sky is dark with them, swooping and circling around, looking for rectories to light on. They settle down on priests like vampire bats."

"They must get damn little blood out of you," Daniel said. "I take my hat off to you: I never saw Delia leave a room so fast!"

"I give them no time at all," the priest said. "I hold the diocesan record for getting rid of women like your sister. More and more of the other priests are coming to me for advice on the subject."

"You'd think they'd know how to handle it for themselves," Daniel said thoughtfully.

"You'd be surprised. It's a question of temperament. Some of them are sentimental, tender-hearted. Sometimes fantastically so. They keep mumbling about Christian charity; I have to point out to them that Christian charity has nothing to do with it. The training is all wrong, of course. The poor lads know nothing about women. The seminary education is at fault there. It teaches them about women, yes, but what kind of women? *Attractive* women, the kind of women who could threaten their celibacy, lead them to concupiscence. The average young priest is adequately prepared for women of some grace, some beauty, some charm. But someone like your sister comes as a complete surprise."

"I'll bet she does," Daniel said.

"Time, experience: they're the only teachers," Father Feeley said. "Through them you eventually develop a technique for dealing with these harpies."

"You've got the technique, all right," Daniel said admiringly. "Biff bang boom, and they're out of the room."

"The frontal assault, yes. Otherwise you live like

[99]

a slave. Well," Father Feeley said, "to other matters. Today's the day?"

"That's right. Tonight's the big showdown."

"They're still determined to get you out?"

Daniel nodded. "They are."

"And you're still determined to stay?"

"I am."

Father Feeley said simply, "Why?"

Daniel stared at him. *"Why?* Because it's my
home, that's why. Every man's got to have a home
at last!"

"Yes yes," Father Feeley said. "A sense of attach-
ment to people, places: I lack it myself. One seems
pretty much like another. And we're all six steps
from the grave in any case. However, if that's what
you want, my best wishes. We're all different. And
so forth."

"By God," Daniel said, still staring at him. "I
swear I don't know what —" He stopped suddenly,
holding up a hand, cautioning silence. He listened,
then looked at the priest, pointed to the door, and
said in a low voice, "Did you hear anything out
there?"

"No no," Father Feeley said. "Nothing at all. Possibly a footstep: normal enough in hallways. Perhaps not even that."

[100]

"Perhaps my eye!" Daniel said. Hurrying over to the door, he stopped in front of it and shouted, "So we've stooped, have we, to eavesdropping on an old man when he makes his holy confession to his priest?"

And then, exactly as he had done earlier in the day with Billy in the room, he flung the door open dramatically; once again, there was no one there. Daniel stepped quickly into the hall and for a moment disappeared. He came back almost immediately, disappointment in his face. He said, "She got away."

"Remarkable," Father Feeley said. "The instinct for melodrama: you either have it or you haven't. I haven't."

"She was there, I tell you!" Daniel said. "Or else the damn maid was, doing her spying for her. You don't know her; she never stops trying. She'd give anything to know my plans."

"Well, it takes all kinds," Father Feeley said. "Humanity in its infinite variety. Most of it highly overrated. And most of it capable of anything. A boundless capacity for lunacy, deceit. It all matters very little. In the long run."

Daniel liked and respected this priest he had known for so many years. Living in increased iso-

lation each year, Father Feeley had for most of his
fellow creatures a feeling which Daniel understood
and found congenial. Not only did he not suffer
fools gladly, he did not suffer them at all. *A real
priest,* Daniel thought admiringly: *they damn
well don't waste his time.* No, there was no guff,
no Come-unto-me-with-your-troubles-and-we'll-all-
have-a-good-boo-hoo-hoo nonsense about Frank
Feeley. If they wanted to cry on Father Feeley's
shoulder, they had first to find Father Feeley — in
itself not always easy. And once they had found
him — well, then the fun began! On the whole,
Daniel considered, he was one priest who was both
a splendid man and who knew which end was up.
And yet, much as he liked him, much as he admired him, there were times — and this was one
of them — when he wondered whether Father
Feeley really understood his problem at all. Not
that he ever actually dismissed it — God knows he
could hardly do that! — but he had a tendency, on
occasion, to treat it as something less than it was.
It was well enough to say that it all mattered very
little in the end, but by God, Daniel thought indignantly, there were some things that mattered
more than others, there were some things that
damn well mattered very much! An old man hav-

ing to scrap like hell to stay in what you might call his own home, for instance: *that* mattered. *That* was no trashy little problem brought in by a rectory nuisance. It was something entirely different. It was something *big.* . . .

Did Father Feeley grasp this? Looking at the priest now, sitting so undisturbed in his chair, Daniel felt, with another and greater spurt of indignation, that he almost certainly did not. With something like despair, Daniel thought that in a way he was unlucky in his friends. They were all right, he would say nothing against them, but what the hell, a man liked to have people around him who knew what he was up against, who could encourage him, who could *appreciate* him. In this sense, of course, Billy was a far better audience than Father Feeley, but here you had to be careful, for Billy took watching. You had to keep your eye on Billy every blessed second, or else — bango! Before you knew it he'd be right up there on the stage with you! Talking. About himself. Whereas Father Feeley, whatever his faults, rarely talked, and when he did he almost never talked about himself. Remembering this, Daniel suddenly felt better, and his thoughts of this old friend grew softer.

A fair man, he liked to give credit where credit was due.

From time to time, in cases which for one reason or another had required Mr. Pomeroy's attention, Tom had served as the old man's junior. He was soon to do so again, and late in the afternoon he went into the senior partner's office with the necessary papers he had prepared. Mr. Pomeroy was small, seventy-five, and spruce; he wore rimless glasses, was covered with liver spots, and had a very long and very thin nose. Like all the old men Tom knew, he was in excellent health. It was with his long nose rather than with his eyes that he seemed to read the papers Tom gave him, stabbing each sentence and snuffling it up with great rapidity. When he had finished he nodded and handed the papers back. "All right," he said. It was his accolade. He handed Tom a sourball from the large apothecary jar on his desk; Tom thought: Bonus.

An hour or so later, in a bar near the office, he was telling the story of this meeting to Mr. Pomeroy's son. Jack Pomeroy was an old friend. They had gone through college and law school together and then, professionally, had parted, for Jack had refused to go into his father's firm.

"Not me," he had said to Tom at the time. "I may not be the smartest lawyer in town, but I'm too smart for that. I know what I'd wind up doing on that team, and just between the two of us, I'm too old to carry pails. No, you go; it's all right for you. You're not his son. You'll work up to a living wage in no time. And on the way say hello to my old man for me. Better pick a summer day to say it; the air gets chilly up there."

That had been twenty years ago. Jack, who drank too much and who was lazy, also had brains; he had done quite well on his own. Old Mr. Pomeroy, who of course knew of his son's friendship with Tom, had never once spoken of him. Jack, on the other hand — or so it seemed to Tom — had long spells in which he spoke of little else but his father. Now, listening to the story, he said, "He's loaded with charm, no? And still pushing those sourballs: isn't it a riot? Not that it matters, but you don't like them, do you?"

"No."

"Neither does he. At least I've never seen him eat one. It's part of his costume, like that fake Abraham Lincoln suit he wears. The old-fashioned counselor. Probity. Tutt and Mr. Tutt. And all that jazz. He's about as homespun as General Dynamics. I can think of a few other parallels there, too."

Tom knew this speech; he said slowly, "I can't figure him out on this one. It has to be something special to get him into court these days. But this isn't special. It isn't anything. It's just a divorce case which might even get fairly dirty before we're through. I was even a little surprised we took it on."

"Ha ha ha," Jack said.

"All right. But the point is that we just don't get into anything like that unless it's worth it."

"I'll buy that," Jack said. "My old man practically invented that high-church dirty pool you fellows play over there, but I don't guess he lets you play it for fun. So what's your problem: you can't figure out the payoff?"

"That's about it. It doesn't make much sense right now. Particularly for your father. I don't get him in this picture at all."

"There's a reason. There's always a reason whenever The Defender of The Poor gets into the game. Try money; that usually works."

"Not here," Jack said. "Well, there's some, but not your father's kind."

"Who's the client?"

"That's a little bit of a surprise, too. It's Charlie

Hamilton. You might keep that under your hat for another day or so."

"Charlie Hamilton. *Our* Charlie Hamilton?"

Tom nodded. Hamilton had been a year ahead of them at college. He had been a campus great, he had been a football star — third-team All American, twice — but after graduation his stature had decreased, and gradually he had slipped out of sight. Until the past week Tom had not heard his name for years.

"Well well well," Jack said. "Charlie Hamilton. He sells cars now, I think. Or he did the last I heard. Anyway, there's no dough there. So *that's* out. And there's no social position, either. Or none to speak of. So that's no good. And . . . who's bringing the action? Charlie?"

"No, the wife."

"Good girl," Jack said approvingly. "Anyone who gives Charlie Hamilton the shove is a friend of mine. The Prince of Turds. Rivaled for sheer turdiness only by one elderly man who for the moment shall be nameless. Who's the wife, by the way? Anyone we know?"

"No one I know. Her name was Beckwith."

Jack sat up straight. "Just try this on for size,"

he said slowly. "It wouldn't be Betsy Beckwith, I suppose."

"I think so, yes. Why: does that mean something?"

"Does it ever. Memories, memories. No kidding: didn't you ever know Betsy?"

Tom shook his head. "No. I missed something: right?"

"Ho ho *ho*. You missed *everything*. But how I'll never know. Betsy was the Great Available. A friend to hundreds, night and day. And she wound up with Charlie Hamilton! Talk about atoning for the sins of your youth! If you'd call them sins. That's what *you* call them, isn't it? Although with Betsy . . . anyway," he said, "that clears up the mystery. About why Dear Old Dad is playing."

"Not to me, it doesn't."

"No? Then you haven't done your homework. You read all the wrong books. I keep telling you that if you're going to work in that bucket shop my old man operates there's only one book you've got to know cold, and that's our own little Blue Book. You've got to know Who's Who and where the bodies are buried. That's all I know, but it's all I need to know. Genealogy is the key to everything in this town. The right kind of genealogy. For ex-

[108]

ample: Betsy Beckwith. Betsy Beckwith's father was General Beckwith, Brigadier General V. C. Beckwith. *Capisce?*"

Tom nodded. "Sure. The man on the horse. In the Memorial Day parades."

"That's right. Far-from-the-Battle-Beckwith. Well, the thing to remember is that the General wasn't just a clown on a horse. He was other things as well. He wasn't a soldier, of course, or anything like that, but he was a very good politician. That's how he got his commission. That, plus the fact that he married a Goodchild; that didn't exactly hurt. Anyway, at one time the General came pretty close to being top banana in Republican politics around here. And at one time John Pomeroy Senior decided to have a fling at Republican politics. He decided to run for governor. Stop me if I'm boring you."

Disregarding this, Tom said, "When did all this happen?"

"Nineteen-twenty-eight. Way back when. You didn't even know any of us in those days, did you? Lucky boy."

Tom had not known them then. The son of Waltzing Daniel Considine, he had met Jack, and Jack's world, later, at a succession of conservative and expensive boarding schools. It was this world in which he now moved comfortably enough, but not quite by instinct. That sometimes, he felt, made a difference.

"So my old man, in that self-effacing way he has, said that if nobody minded he thought he'd become governor. But unfortunately somebody did mind. General Beckwith. There was a hell of a fight, and the great trial lawyer really pulled out all the stops. He had a lot of very powerful supporters, not because they liked him, of course, but because he'd kept so many of them out of the can. But he got licked all the same. He started out fine, but then the Beckwiths *and* the Goodchilds began to turn on the heat, and that fixed that. By the time the convention rolled around, Big Daddy was a dead duck. Real dead. Forever. He never ran for anything again. Unless I'm wrong, he never even voted again. But from time to time he may have given a passing thought to General Beckwith. And the General's family. As you may have noticed."

It was an explanation. Was it possible? Probable? Tom thought about this for no more than a few seconds, and then said softly, "Poor Betsy Beckwith."

"Poor Betsy Beckwith," Jack agreed. "She was a

naughty little girl in her day, and guess who's going to find out all about *that*? Whether you do your
part or not. No, she hasn't got a prayer. He'll get
her on the stand and spin her dizzy. That soft
nasal whine will peel the skin right off her bones.
Fortunately I won't be there to see it. For some
reason I've never gone to see my old man in court.
Everyone tells me he's marvelous, but of course I
have an advantage that they haven't. I've caught
his act at home."

For the past half hour he had been drinking
quite steadily. Now he ordered another drink,
shrugged, and said, "I'll tell you what: let's change
the subject. Is that conceivable?"

They talked for perhaps another fifteen minutes
before Tom decided to go; he left Jack sitting there,
alone and drinking quietly. This was the way he
finished each day.

Outside, Tom thought of going home; the
thought was not attractive, and so he returned to
his office. On the way, thinking about his talk with
Jack, he realized with something of a shock that
this was the only meeting or conversation he had
had all day in which his father had not been mentioned. Yet, curiously, nothing in the day had made
him think of his father more. . . .

[111]

five

IN Daniel's room the two old men had been talking, mostly about Daniel, and not entirely to Daniel's satisfaction. Still, he did not complain. Father Feeley was Father Feeley: he knew that; he told himself that the priest was too old to change, and besides, in a sense it was all just killing time: the real thing was yet to come. Clearly, they were waiting, and it was Father Feeley who at last pulled out his pocket watch, looked at it, and said abruptly, "Where are the others?"

"Billy's never on time," Daniel said. "But Gottlieb should be here by now. He's a very punctual man."

"I like Gottlieb," Father Feeley said. "I've never met a sadder man."

"Oh, he's sad, all right," Daniel said. "They come no sadder than Gottlieb."

"What's the tragedy there?" the priest said. "Domestic?"

"Very domestic. He was a very domestic man. His family meant a hell of a lot to him. He was like me in a way, except that he got along with his wife. Anyways, it was the wife that started it all. She ran off with a band leader."

"Good God in heaven," Father Feeley said. "*Which* band leader?"

"I don't know that you'd remember him. Lester Espinosa."

"Espinosa," Father Feeley said thoughtfully. "Espinosa. Tall, dark, thick-lipped? The face of a degenerate? Played in the pit of the old Orpheum?"

"The very man," Daniel said. "Lester Espinosa."

"Of course I remember him," the priest said. "He's unforgettable. A dreadful man, even for a musician. Virtually an animal. No one could run off with Espinosa."

"Well, Gottlieb's wife did," Daniel said. "And without so much as a word of warning. One night Gottlieb came home for dinner and what did he find but his wife gone and a little note on the bureau saying, 'Goodbye forever, Gottlieb. I've just run off with Lester Espinosa.' "

"Fantastic," Father Feeley said. " 'Goodbye forever, Gottlieb!' What a note! Cheap, vulgar, theatrical: no wonder the man was offended!"

"Oh yes. That, plus the fact she was gone. But that's not the worst. Not by a long shot. After she left he was lonesome, being so much of a family man, so he went out to California to stay with his son. The son lives in Hollywood; he does something in one of the picture studios — I don't know just what. Anyways, Gottlieb went out there to live with him, but in two months he was back. And sadder than before."

"I'm surprised he lasted that long," said Father Feeley. "The place is a swamp. Full of thieves, perverts and crooners. No sane man could stay there overnight."

"Well, it wasn't the place so much as the son," Daniel said. "And the son's new wife. They belong to a crazy bunch out there that had wild parties every night, and Gottlieb likes to go to bed by nine. He never got any sleep; there were always strange women crashing through his bedroom yelling, 'Is this the way to the toilet?' or 'Did I leave my pocketbook in here?' And then the son's new wife was a big redhead about six feet high that dressed in a cowboy suit. She kept on telling Gottlieb to call her 'Tex.' Well, one night —"

And once more he stopped, held up his hand, and listened; he said to the priest, "Did you hear anything?"

"No," Father Feeley said firmly. "I heard nothing. Go on with your story."

Daniel listened for a moment more, then, apparently satisfied, shrugged and went back to the priest. "Well . . . where was I, anyways?"

"Describing a redheaded savage," Father Feeley said.

"Ah. The son's wife. Well, the two of them did a terrible thing to Gottlieb. They made fun of him. They gave a party one night, and told him it was for him. And when he walked into the room it was already full of people, waiting for him to show up. And what was the first thing he saw but a little ape, sitting on a chair at the other side of the room, and dressed exactly like him! They'd got him from a zoo, you see. He was wearing a little suit just like Gottlieb's, and the same color shirt, and even the same kind of glasses. They'd even slipped a special kind of bald wig over his head so he'd be bald like Gottlieb. So all the people laughed when Gottlieb came into the room and saw the ape. But Gottlieb didn't laugh. He turned right around and left, and the next day he came home."

"Yes, yes, of course," the priest said. "You can't remain in a community where you've been successfully impersonated by a monkey."

"So that's why he was sadder than before," Daniel said. "His wife run off with a band leader, his son gone crazy in Hollywood. Oh, I tell you, a thing like that did something to him. It left him sour on show business for good."

"Show business?" Father Feeley said, in some surprise. "I never thought of Gottlieb in that connection."

"Well, that's because you only know him today," Daniel said. "Years ago it was a different story. Years ago Gottlieb was a great man for the theater. There wasn't a vaudeville show came to town he didn't see. He loved vaudeville. And if I played any place within a hundred miles of here, Gottlieb would be right there in the front row. Next to you, he was my biggest fan."

"Well, I was your fan for an entirely different reason," Father Feeley said. "I liked *you:* I never liked vaudeville. By and large it seemed to me a collection of absurd people: middle-aged idiots with dyed hair singing love songs, Chinese laundrymen throwing Indian clubs at each other, malformed women doing indecent gymnastics. Farcical nonentities, all of them. You were an exception, Daniel. It always seemed to me that your performance was a marvelous burlesque of your co-workers. Consciously or unconsciously, you were indicating contempt for the whole imbecilic milieu. It was the kind of performance a sane man could enjoy."

"Well," Daniel said, "I never bothered to figure it out. Like that or any other way. I just did it. I suppose people came to see me for all sorts of reasons. I never gave a damn so long as they came. And when they came, I gave them what they came for: the old dance."

Rising, he broke into just the beginning of his dance. He stopped, and said to the priest, "The funny thing was, I never changed it. The others were always changing their act, but I never did. Oh, sometimes they asked me to, but I always said —"

Suddenly, and once more, he held up his hand; Father Feeley said impatiently, "Now now, Daniel! Enough is enough!"

"Ssshh!" Daniel said. "Be quiet: I heard something!"

And he had, for now there was a knock on the door. It was a soft, apologetic knock; it was also the code knock.

"What the hell did I tell you?" Daniel said triumphantly. "That'll be Gottlieb."

He went quickly to the door and opened it. Standing there, looking at him, was a small, elderly bald man. He was carefully and expensively dressed; he was unmistakably Jewish; there was about him an air of almost radiant dejection. His hands hung down by his sides; as the door opened, he raised his right hand an inch or so in greeting.

Daniel said, "Ah, Gottlieb!"

Still standing at the door, Gottlieb said, in a soft unhappy voice, "I'm not intruding?"

"No no," Daniel said. "Come in, come in. We've been waiting a hell of a while for you."

"I would have been here earlier," Gottlieb said, entering, "but my car: it suffered a breakdown. The radiator cap blew off and almost hit a person." He advanced and shook hands with the priest. "It's a pleasure to see you again, Father."

"You look well, Mr. Gottlieb," Father Feeley said. "Alert. Vigorous. In spite of the heat."

"I'm alive," Gottlieb said, shrugging. "Whether that's good or bad, who's to say?"

"Sit down, Gottlieb," Daniel said. "Sit down and join the party. We're just waiting for Billy."

"To tell you the honest truth," Gottlieb said, seating himself, "aside from being alive, I don't feel so good today. I just came from an old friend.

I saw him yesterday afternoon, he was on top of the world. I saw him this afternoon, he was stretched out in a coffin. What happened was this: he died. A clot."

"Tragic," Father Feeley said. "On the brain, I presume?"

"On the brain," Gottlieb said, nodding. "He died from a clot on the brain. Forty-eight hours ago this very minute that man was out on the golf course. Every day of his life he played a game of golf. He would have been a champion player if he didn't have such short arms. And forty-eight hours ago that man played eighteen holes of golf. He shot an eighty-three from the back tees. Now he's dead from a clot. Gentlemen, I tell you this: a thing like that, it makes a man think. Where are we going? What are we doing? Why?"

Daniel said slowly, "Would that be Glickman, I wonder?"

"Nobody else but," Gottlieb said. "It was Glickman. My old friend Artie Glickman."

"I saw in the papers he died," Daniel said, "but it didn't say what he died of."

"A clot," Gottlieb said. "He died from a clot. And if you asked me yesterday afternoon who would be the last man I know to die from a clot,

I swear to God I would have said one name. I would have said the name of Artie Glickman."

Daniel said, "You would of been wrong."

Gottlieb said, "I would have been wrong. About that I wouldn't care so much. A man is wrong, so he's wrong. It happened before, it could happen again. But about my old friend Artie Glickman — that I can't get over so easy. And on top of everything else, you know what they're doing on him? A cremation!"

"Ah, that's a bad business," Daniel said disapprovingly.

"Forty-eight hours ago he shoots an eighty-three from the back tees," Gottlieb said, "and tomorrow he's a little pile of ashes you could put in a coffee cup. Gentlemen, that's the story of us all."

"Dust to dust," said Father Feeley. "And so forth."

"But why the cremation I'll never know," Gottlieb said. "Maybe because he wasn't such a religious person. You know what Artie Glickman's religion was? *Golf*. The game of golf was his only religion. I don't shock you by saying that, Father?"

"No no," Father Feeley said. "Not at all. We live in a crazy world. All things are possible."

Gottlieb said mournfully, "So now — ashes. A

stranger could walk into that room and say to himself: 'What was here before these ashes? A cigar? A stick of wood? The *New York Times*?' In a million years he couldn't guess they came from a lovely human being by the name of Artie Glickman. And tomorrow morning at eleven o'clock A.M. they put those ashes on a plane — a Piper Cub — and they scatter him down all over the Red Cross. His favorite charity."

"With a little note," Daniel said, "saying, 'He gave for the last time.'"

"Daniel!" Gottlieb said reprovingly. "A deceased person!"

"I know, I know. I'm sorry, Gottlieb," Daniel said. "All the same, it's a hell of a way to go. All burnt up and ready for the ashtray. Still, they do a lot of that stuff in other countries. India's a great place for all that nonsense. One time I played India for a couple of months and I never saw the like of them for burning people up. There's times the whole damn place is a torch. They're little fellers, you know: all skin and bones. I suppose they burn very fast. That may be it. Anyways, a man would hardly dare to lie down and close his eyes for fear someone would put a match to him. It's kind of like a hobby with them. By God, I was never so glad to get out of a place in my life!"

"A strange land," Father Feeley said. "Contradictions of all sorts. Spiritual, yet sensual, the people half mad with drugs. And of course theologically a mess. I wouldn't have thought they could grasp your act at all, Daniel."

"No, well, I don't think they did, much," Daniel said. "I did as well as anyone, but they're not used to high-class entertainment over there. All they've got is snake charmers and double-jointed dancers and fake magicians. When you get a lot of Indians looking at you, you've got a bad audience. They might giggle and titter a little, but on the whole they're a dull crowd. No, I wouldn't go back to play India for love or money!"

"I still can't get over it," Gottlieb said. "My old friend Artie Glickman: here today and gone tomorrow! A nice man who wouldn't harm a dog. All alone in his hotel room at night, watching a Wally Beery movie on the television, and — bam! A clot. Ten minutes later it's goodbye Artie."

"That's a queer one," Daniel said. "Dying, I mean, in the middle of a Wally Beery movie. I never heard of that before. I used to know Wally Beery years ago. Not well, you know, but we used to meet and say hello now and then. He was a hell of an actor. No man ever lived that could scratch himself the way Wally Beery could."

"Dead now himself, isn't he?" Father Feeley asked.

"Oh yes, a good while now," Daniel said. "I forget just when it was."

"Nineteen-forty-nine," Gottlieb said. "In April."

"Leave it to Gottlieb," Daniel said admiringly. "If you want to know a fact about show business — names, dates, or places — there's the greatest man in the country for you."

Gottlieb shook his head. "No. No more, Daniel. Nowadays I take no interest. What you're speaking of is Gottlieb years ago. Before my misfortune. Then, maybe what you said is right. But since my misfortune an atom bomb could go off and blow all the theaters in the world sky-high and to sawdust, and you know what I'd do? I'd go right on reading my paper. If I so much as said one word, that word would be 'Good riddance.' I'm not shocking you, Father? You're not looking at me and saying, 'There sits Gottlieb, a beast in human form'?"

"No no," Father Feeley said. "I frequently feel the same way. Most of the time, in fact."

"And yet," Gottlieb said, "years ago, if anybody

had come up to me and said I'd feel like this some-day, you know what I would have done? I would have looked him right in the eye and said, 'You are a liar, my friend.' It all goes to show you: we never know. What can we be sure of? Nothing. I tell you, gentlemen, it makes a man think. Artie Glickman dying like that, my misfortune: Why? You're a man of the cloth, Father: why should such terrible things happen?"

"God knows," said Father Feeley. "I don't. We see through a glass darkly. And so forth."

"You're acquainted with the nature of my mis-fortune, Father?" Gottlieb said.

"Yes yes," the priest said. "Daniel told me. The faithless wife, the serpent son. Tragic. Moving. My sympathy."

"Thank you," Gottlieb said. He paused, then said, "You know, I'm glad Daniel informed you, Father. Because I couldn't do it myself, not for a million dollars. Eleven years ago my misfortune happened to me, and to this day I still can't talk about it to another human being. You understand how that could be, Father?"

"Yes, yes. Scars, I imagine. Plus a natural deli-cacy."

"You're absolutely right," Gottlieb said. "So

you'll excuse me if I don't talk about it now?"

"Gladly, gladly," Father Feeley said. "I'm all for reticence. The sorrow borne in silence: we see far too little of that today."

Gottlieb said, "The funny thing is, it's so fresh in my mind it's just like it was yesterday. When it happened, I mean. Driving back to the house from my business, you know, the same time as always: five-thirty, five-forty-five. I parked the car — a Dodge — I opened the front door — there's a special lock I had put on so my wife wouldn't be afraid: she's a very nervous woman — and inside everything looked the same. The big clock in the hall going tick tock, tick tock, a bowl of nice fruit on the table, a vase of fresh daisies on the stand by the telephone. What a flower lover she was, Father! Fresh ones every day. So everything looked the same, everything even *smelled* the same. There was no big voice that came to me and said, 'Starting tonight, Al Gottlieb, your whole life goes to smash!' I didn't even get a hint."

"Just a note," Daniel said.

"Just a note," Gottlieb said. "A piece of paper. Thin, like tissue paper. A piece of paper that said only one thing: Goodbye. My wife was gone. Sarah Gottlieb, wife of Al, was gone with the wind."

Daniel said, "And a damn bad wind at that. Named Lester Espinosa."

"What does it all mean?" Gottlieb asked, looking imploringly at the priest. "A middle-aged lady, she's got a nice home, a hard-working husband who loves her, she wants anything, she lifts her finger and she's got it! And all this she leaves for a . . . for a what? I'll tell you for a what: for a flashy dope-taker and a bum! Again I ask you, gentlemen: What's the answer to a thing like that?"

"Concealed from human view," Father Feeley said. "We live surrounded by mysteries. And scoundrels."

"I've met bad people in my time," Daniel said, "but Lester Espinosa was one of the worst. I'll never forgive that man."

"Loyalty, loyalty," Father Feeley said. "Commendable. Fine."

"You'd come out onto the Orpheum stage, you know," Daniel continued, "and with the first step you could tell something was wrong. The music sounded all off key and the wrong beat: you could break a leg dancing to it. And you'd look down into the pit and who'd be there, leading the band, but that damned idiot, grinning at everybody, and blowing away on that fake gold clarinet! I'd hate to tell you how many times he nearly ruined my act. After a week in the same theater with him I was lucky I had any act left at all. Oh yes, that's the kind of a man Lester Espinosa was. You couldn't forgive a man like that."

"And my wife, Daniel," Gottlieb said. "What he did to my wife."

"That too, of course," Daniel said. "Yes, yes."

"So she left me, Father," Gottlieb said, turning back to Father Feeley. "My wife for thirty years left me and she didn't come back. Not even once. And not only that, six months later, my own son, Al Gottlieb Junior, my own Sonny Boy — but about him I can't make myself say a single word."

"No no," the priest said. "Don't try, don't try."

"He broke my heart, Father," Gottlieb said. "What was left of my heart to break, that boy broke it. I raised him up to be a real good boy. He went to nice schools, he played baseball with the other kids, I gave him every advantage. He was a real All American boy — a *good* boy. In the war he was almost a hero. He comes home from the war, all of a sudden he decided California, Here I Come, he leaves his old Mom and Dad and goes out to Hollywood. He becomes a picture agent,

he becomes a crazy man. He marries one girl; it's
no good. He marries another girl, a giant. She
thinks she's a cowboy. He changes his name. Al
Gottlieb Junior: what's wrong with that for a
name? It's a good name, an honest name, a name
he should be proud of. But look it up in the phone
book out there, you won't find it. He's got a new
name now, Father. You know what it is? La-
France! That's not crazy enough, you know what
his first name is? Chips! I said to him, 'What kind
of a name is that? Tell me one person in the
whole wide world who's called a Chips!' 'I am,
Poppa,' he said. 'Out here everybody calls me
Chips.' So my boy, my only son, my Al Gottlieb
Junior, is now a Chips LaFrance!"

"Absurd," Father Feeley said. "Ludicrous. And
yet typical: we live in the midst of a roaring farce."

"What happened to my nice good boy?" asked
Gottlieb, throwing out his arms. "He's gone crazy
in the head, he thinks he's a big shot. He said to
me out there, 'Poppa, I might go to live in England.' I said, 'Why England, in the name of God?
What's the matter with the good old U.S.A.?' He
said, 'Poppa, you don't understand: for what I'm
doing here, in England I could get made a knight.
A *Sir!*' I said to him, 'Sonny, go take a cold shower;

you're a crazy person. What an ambition you've got in your head! How could they make you a Sir, they wouldn't even know what to call you? Sir Chips LaFrance? Or Sir Al Gottlieb Junior? Don't talk like this to people, Sonny, or they'll come for you with the doctors!' "

"No no, that's perfectly normal conversation out there," Father Feeley said. "Your son's in complete rapport with his environment. They all talk like that in Hollywood. Sanity is the stranger."

"I wouldn't care if he was only crazy," Gottlieb said. "You've got a crazy boy, you can take care of him. But a *cruel* boy: that's something different. He's a cruel son, Father. My Sonny grew up to be a cruel person. He's got no respect any more; he plays bad jokes on his old Dad. What he did to me you wouldn't believe any boy would do to his father. He gave a party and hired a little gorilla to look like me. I never thought my Sonny would do a thing like that to me. So I came away from him. He didn't want me, so I came away."

"There's no getting around it, Gottlieb," Daniel said. "Your family could of been better to you."

"A family: what is it?" asked Gottlieb. "Gentlemen, I'll tell you: a family is something to punch you in the nose. Hard. Twenty years ago you could

shoot me dead before I'd say a terrible thing like
that. Today, it should be on billboards. In big black
letters. Look at my family: my wife, my Sonny.
In one small year they took all the joy from my
life. You wouldn't believe it, Father, but Al Gottlieb was once a gay person. Always whistling, always a little song, always going to see the shows.
Walking along the street, I'd see a boy, a little kid,
a total stranger, crying, I'd go up to him and say,
'Cheer up, sonny: whatever you're crying about,
believe me, it's not worth it. Here's a dime: go get
yourself a chocolate ice cream cone. With jim-
mies.' Now, today, if I see a little kid like that,
I walk right by him. I feel like saying to him,
'You're crying, so cry. All through your whole life
you'll get plenty to cry about, so go ahead: get a
good head start.' That's what I feel like telling that
little kid, Father. And that's what my family did
to me. They made of me a sad man. A bad cynic.
That's what families do to people."

"Yes, yes," Father Feeley said. "Well, we all
change. I don't think it's a question of family entirely. Disappointment, discouragement with humanity at large: that comes with age, experience,
wisdom. I myself have a small tendency in that
direction."

[130]

"And not all families are like yours, Gottlieb,"
Daniel said. "I don't say anything about the wives;
God knows there's loads of people that get a bad
shake in that department. But the sons are different. Not all sons turn on their fathers. Not if
you know how to handle them right."

"Daniel, we've known each other a long time,"
Gottlieb said solemnly. "You'll excuse me for saying something to you? Something I wanted to say
to you before? Something I want to say to you
now, today of all days?"

"What's that?" Daniel said.

"*Watch out.*"

Daniel stared at him. "Watch out? What the
hell is that supposed to mean? Watch out for
what?"

"Watch out for young people," Gottlieb said.
"They're all the same. I speak from experience."

"What young people?" Daniel said. "Are you
talking about Tom? My own flesh and blood?"

Gottlieb said, "All I say, Daniel, not naming any
names, is your own flesh and blood — believe me,
they can be the worst. You love them, you trust
them, and one day — boom! And you don't even
know what hit you. Believe me, Daniel, I know
what I'm talking about!"

[131]

"You know what you're talking about for *you*, Gottlieb," Daniel said. "But what the hell has that got to do with *me*? I tell you, if my son ever tried to pull anything like that on me, he'd damn soon —"

But once again he was interrupted, and again by a knock on the door. It was not the code knock but a loud and indiscriminate banging, and Daniel, snapping around to the door, cried angrily, "Leave us alone! Can't a man have any peace and privacy when he's talking to his friends? Go away!"

But the voice which answered was a familiar one. "Open up, Daniel," it said. "Open up, my dear man. It's Billy."

"Good God in heaven!" muttered Daniel, jumping up and going to the door. Opening it, he said, "Why the hell don't you use the knock, Billy? What do you suppose I have one for if nobody uses it?"

"My apologies, my dear man," Billy said, entering the room, his satchel in his hand. "I'm sorry: I was in such a hurry to get here the knock completely slipped my mind. I was out on a last-minute call, you see: a matter of life and death." As casually as he had early that morning, he now threw the satchel onto Daniel's bed. "Life and death," he said. "Oh yes. It's all around us every day. Hello, Father. Hello, Gottlieb, my dear man."

Father Feeley nodded, pleasantly enough, and Gottlieb raised a hand in silent greeting. Daniel, mollified by the medical explanation, pointed to the satchel, and said, "Why the hell don't you get a new bag? That one's all worn out. It's got rips in the corners. Look, you've got something sticking out now!"

Billy looked; he said, "That's nothing, my dear man: just an old sock. I'm taking some things down to the Chinaman to get them washed. I didn't have time to get over there on account of my patient."

"Who is he?" Daniel said. "Anyone I know?"

"I hardly think so, my dear man. He's over in the East End: a poor old devil of an Italian with a bad bladder. Scientifically speaking, it's the classical bladder case. In the language of the layman, he can't do Number One."

"Is he all swelled up?" Daniel said.

"Tight as a drum," Billy said. "You tap that old Italian's abdomen with the tips of your fingers and you get a sound you can hear two blocks away! The Official Doctors are all for the operation, of course: the same old ignorant knife-happy crowd. Fortunately the family called me in on

time. I reassured the man. He was in a panic till
I got to him. 'Forget the knife, my dear man,' I
told him. 'I wouldn't allow that gang to even cut
my fingernails. No, we'll treat you medically. Wonder drugs are the answer. *New* wonder drugs! The
very latest thing! The bladder's friend, they call
them. Oh yes,' I said to that man, 'calm down and
forget your troubles. We'll have you playing leap-
frog in a week!' "

"Well, if that's what he wants to do, good luck
to him," Daniel said. "Still, the family was damn
lucky they got on to you when they did. How did
they do that, anyways?"

"Through the milkman," Billy said. "I once
cured his sister of an unpleasant nasal disorder:
the double snuffles. Ever since then he's spread the
word around." He reached into a pants pocket and
produced, for general inspection, a handful of
large capsules. "Here they are: right off the boat
from the Swedes! The newest wonder drugs of all!
I'll slip a few of these to our friend the Italian,
and in less than forty-eight hours that man will
be a human hydrant!"

"Excuse me, Billy," Gottlieb said, peering at the
capsules, "but these are what you're giving to that
old gentleman? Just like this?"

"Yes, yes, the very latest thing," Billy said. Generously, he held out his open hand. "Have one, my dear man. Help yourself! Just in case! At your age you never know!"

"No no," Gottlieb said hastily, backing away. "No, thank you just the same. But if you'll forgive me saying so, Billy, is that so sanitary? Right from your pocket like that, I mean? Look: you see what they've got on them? Lint!"

"It couldn't matter less, my dear man," Billy said. "Wonder drugs like these destroy the deadliest germs in a matter of seconds; what chance do you think lint has against them?"

"Farce, farce!" Father Feeley said suddenly. "We live in the midst of a musical comedy!"

Gottlieb turned to the priest, his face polite and slightly puzzled. "What Billy's saying, Father: you don't subscribe?"

"Subscribe!" Father Feeley said. "Good God in heaven! The jungle pharmacist, pure and simple. Pep pills from a pants pocket! And poor warped simpletons actually take them and yowl for more. We're all two steps from the zoo!"

Billy said equably, "Father and I, my dear man, have a few small differences on scientific matters. He once preached a sermon against me."

"It had no effect, of course," Father Feeley said. "Predictable: nobody listened."

"But you're not angry?" Gottlieb said. "I mean, personally it's all right? No hard feelings?"

"No no, my dear man," Billy said. "I've known Father here all my life. I understand his position perfectly. What he says he has to say. The Church is a miracle of organization, but they're a moss-back crowd in matters of science. Look what they did to my colleague Galileo!"

"Galileo!" Father Feeley said. "My colleague Galileo! The perfect equation! The whole thing's a madman's paradise!"

"Well, good luck to the Italian and his bladder," Daniel said briefly. This discussion had ceased to please him. Politely, he had asked a simple question; he had provoked a debate. A foolish debate, a debate which had no connection with anything that mattered, with anything he planned to do. It was Billy again; he knew that. He said loudly, "What we were talking about, Billy, was young people, and the way to handle them. Like Gottlieb's boy."

Gottlieb said, "You're acquainted with my misfortune, Billy?"

"Oh yes, my dear man," Billy said. "I know all

about that one. A fascinating case, clinically speaking. The genetically twisted offspring. Or, in the language of the layman, the foul-ball son."

"Gottlieb here was trying to tell me all young people are like that," Daniel said. "We got talking about Tom and me."

"Daniel, for all the world I wouldn't say a word against your own son personally," Gottlieb said. "For all I know he's a marvelous young person who loves his old Dad. For all I know he's a good boy who would cut off his right arm at the shoulder before he would make his old Dad feel bad. That could be. All I'm saying, Daniel, speaking generally and from my own experience, is that today young people want to say only one thing to their old folks: Goodbye Charlie!"

"Well, here's one Charlie they won't say goodbye to," Daniel said grimly. "I can promise you that!"

"You'll excuse me for reminding you, Daniel," Gottlieb said apologetically, "but — *they already did.* Four weeks ago tonight, in this very house, what did he say to you, your own boy? 'Be my guest'? No. You know what he said, Daniel. He said one thing. He said to get out. Just like my Sonny."

"No, not just like your Sonny!" Daniel said. "Not by a damn sight. There's a hell of a difference there, Gottlieb, and the difference is this: *I don't let them get away with it*. Listen to me: I don't say you're wrong about what young people will *try* to do. They're a selfish lot, even the best of them. What I say is, you're wrong because you let them do it. And by God, I don't! When it comes to that kind of scrapping, I know a thing or two myself!"

"The very reason we're here, my dear man!" Billy cried. "The very reason we're on tap. To see the preview of the battle plan! A demonstration, we might say, for the privileged few."

"And I'll give you one," Daniel said. "I promised I would, and I will!" He rose now and stood slightly apart from them, the entertainer before the audience. "Billy," he said, "before I start anything, take a look at that door like a good feller, will you? See that no one's hanging around."

"Little pitchers have big ears, is that it, Daniel?" Billy said, walking over to the door.

"They have damn big ears in this house," Daniel said, "and they're flapping all the time, I can tell you that!"

Billy opened the door and stuck his head out into the hall; Daniel called loudly, "Well, what about it, Billy? Is there any spy out there, as usual?"

"No no, my dear man," Billy said, coming back in. "Not a sight, not a sound. No one was there."

"Oh, she's fast on her feet, I'll say that for her," Daniel said.

"Act one, scene one," Father Feeley said. "The stage is set. The feminine spy. Fast and furtive. Still, it's all possible, I imagine. Anything is."

"It's a damn sight more than possible, it's a fact," Daniel said. "You'd find that out if you lived here instead of in that rectory you keep locked and bolted like a fort so no woman like her can get within ten miles of you."

"Normal defenses, nothing more," said Father Feeley.

"Excuse me, Daniel," Gottlieb said suddenly. "For all the world I wouldn't rush you, but inside an hour I'm expected in town. An appointment. Artie Glickman's sister is crying: she needs a shoulder."

"Yes yes, Daniel, let the performance begin," Billy said. "Too much suspense is bad for the valves. We're all eyes and ears."

"Well, I won't go through the whole thing for you," Daniel explained. "I don't want to take the edge off. And I don't want to get all tired out in rehearsal. But I'll give you enough so you'll get the idea, all right." He paused and stood before them, dramatically motionless; he felt the three men fixed on him; he had their attention. "First of all," he said slowly, "you know what's already happened. What the both of them said to me one month ago."

"Background material, my dear man," Billy said, a trifle impatiently. "The ultimatum is familiar to us all."

"All right," Daniel said flatly. "So you all know that. Well, here's what you don't know. Every night since then Tom's been coming to my door, and knocking on it, and asking me how I am. And do you know what I said back to him? In the whole month? *Not a word.* Not a single blessed word!"

"Oh my my!" Billy said. "Marvelous! The touch of a master! Silence is golden! And what does he say to that, my dear man?"

"Nothing. He doesn't talk much anyways, you know. He's quiet. Sometimes you can't get a word out of him. And when I don't say anything to him, there's nothing he can say back to me. Even if he wanted to. So he goes away. But here's the point:

he goes away thinking. And that's been going on every night for a solid month now. But tonight when he comes to the door and knocks, things are going to be different."

"Tonight, Daniel," Billy cried, "you'll open the door! You'll *ouvrez la porte,* as the French say. It comes to about the same thing."

"Good God in heaven," Father Feeley said. "Continue, Daniel."

"Well, I'll open the door, you know," Daniel said, "and I'll just stand there. But here's the *way* I'll stand." And now, facing them, he seemed to slump, to curve, to collapse partially, and in this way he appeared to be suddenly smaller, defenseless, and even wistful. "Like this, you see. I'll just stand there like this, looking at him. And he'll just stand there, looking at me."

"Moving, my dear man!" Billy said, impressed. "Deeply moving. Standing there face to face."

Father Feeley said, "The common position, of course. When two people meet."

"Just looking," Daniel said again. He gave no sign of having heard Father Feeley. His voice now had a dreamy, private quality, as if he were thinking instead of speaking, addressing himself rather than the other three. "And what'll go through his head right then and there I don't know for sure, but I can make a guess. A damn good guess. Every night for a month I worked on him. Every night for a month I wouldn't speak to him. Every night for a month I wouldn't open the door to him so he could see me. And now he sees me, and sees the way I am, and how will he feel? I think he might damn well feel one way: *ashamed!*"

"Daniel Daniel Daniel!" Gottlieb said despairingly. "What is he, this boy: a Dr. Schweitzer?"

Daniel did not answer; he put up a hand for silence, and continued. "Yes, he'll be ashamed. And he'll say to himself, 'What am I doing? This is my *Dad*. He's my Dad that put me through good schools, that gave me everything I ever wanted, that made me what I am. And now he's an old man and a sick man, and what does he want from me? Not a damn thing in the whole wide world but one little room where he can spend the rest of his days near the only boy he ever had. That's the only thing he ever asked me for, and what did I say to him? I said Out. O-u-t. That's what I said to him! I said it four weeks ago. And now I see him standing here in the doorway, my own Dad, looking at me like this — *can I still say it to him tonight?*' "

This last interrogation was barely whispered; Daniel stopped, and stood before his audience, waiting. There was a respectful silence, broken by Billy.

"Oh, powerful, Daniel!" he said. "Highly powerful! In the language of the layman, a blow to the belly-button!"

"Yes, yes," Father Feeley said. "Rhetoric, of course. Nicely constructed, well-delivered."

Gottlieb looked perplexed; he said, "Excuse me, Daniel, but — *this* is what you're going to do to-night?"

"It's a part of it, yes," Daniel said. "Why?"

"But Daniel," Gottlieb said unhappily. "This boy of yours — a lovely boy and all that, I don't say he isn't — you really think he's going to say, 'Poppa, I'm all wrong, I take it back'? Just because you stand there looking *sad*? Believe me, Daniel, forget it. Take it from an expert: there's nobody that looks sadder than me, and where did it get me? My Sonny stuck a knife in my heart. Young people don't respect sadness, Daniel. They don't know what it is. They've got no experience. You give them a sad look, you waste a sad look, that's all."

"Now, wait a minute," Daniel said. "Hold on —"

"You think I'm a prejudiced person on account

of my misfortune?" Gottlieb said. "Ask Father here: a neutral person. By his religion he's not allowed to have a young boy who could do what my Sonny did to me." He turned to the priest and asked, "What about it, Father? What we just saw now from Daniel: you think it's something good?"

"Fascinating," Father Feeley said. "Faultless in its way. Technically superb. Full of bathos, sentimentality: a caricature of dejection."

"But the boy, Father," Gottlieb said. "You think it could change the boy?"

"Oh no no. I wouldn't think it would have the slightest effect on the boy. In my experience," the priest said, "the young are entirely impervious to that sort of appeal."

"You see, Daniel?" Gottlieb said, turning back to Daniel in melancholy triumph. "You see what Father said? Listen to me. You've got a grown boy, he's made up his mind to tell you Goodbye Charlie, he's got a wife behind him giving him little kicks so he should tell you faster. And for this you're going to look *sad*? Excuse me, Daniel, but it's like a man runs up to you on the street yelling, 'Hurry up, hurry up, the whole city's catching scarlet fever! A real epidemic!' And you say to him, 'Who's worried? I already got a handkerchief.'"

Daniel said again, "Will you wait a minute —"

"Daniel, as a medical man I'm forced to agree with our friends here," Billy said. "Your powerful performance was unforgettable, of course, but with a boy like yours it would all go down the sink. Scientifically speaking, we might say that your chances are one in a thousand. But cheer up, Daniel! We never know about a thing like this. Queer things happen every day that even the best of us can't explain. And why? *Because we just don't know.* They're what we might call Beyond the Realm of Science. They're more in Father's department. I'll tell you what, my dear man: I wouldn't be surprised if Father here got down on his knees for an hour or so for you, something might not happen to your boy, maybe at the very moment you were talking to him. Something to sap his resistance. A spasm of the intestines, maybe. That can be highly painful. He could go soft as a grape; he wouldn't have the strength to say no to you! He might even burst into a Niagara of sobbing tears! Oh yes, Daniel, I'm a man of medicine, but I'm a big enough man to say this to you: When Science fails, call on Father Feeley!"

"Here here here!" Father Feeley said sharply. "That's enough of that nonsense!"

"Don't underestimate the power of prayer, Father!" Billy warned. "I've seen too much of it!"

"DAMN IT TO HELL, WILL YOU WAIT A MINUTE!" Daniel shouted. They all stopped, startled; Daniel regarded them grumpily. "Did you come over here to see what I was going to do, or to argue amongst yourselves?" he asked. "Now for the love of God will you be quiet and let me get in a word edgewise. What the hell is all the fuss about, anyways? What I showed you is just a *part* of it. Just a little something I might begin with. I know damn well nothing like that by itself will do the trick! What d'ye think I am, an idiot or something?"

"Ah, that's better, Daniel," Gottlieb said. "You've got something else: that relieves me."

"Reinforcements from the rear, my dear man," said Billy. "The secret of every successful commander. Look at Napoleon! Look at Bismarck!"

"Both defeated, of course," Father Feeley said. "Ultimately. Still, reserve strength: always wise. Ammunition rather than sentiment. The human animal being what it is."

"What I'll do," Daniel explained, "is this. We'll both be at the door, saying nothing, but looking at each other. I'll step to one side, and I'll ask

him in." And now, in illustration, he accompanied
his words with a pantomime of what was to come:
he stepped aside, beckoned slowly with one hand,
and pointed to the center of the room; he said,
"He'll come in and he'll stand there. Or maybe
he'll sit down. But I'll stay right here, not moving.
I'll close the door behind me, but I'll stand right
here. And we'll start to talk a little. Or *I'll* talk;
he says damn little anyways. He's a listener. So
I'll talk. And I'll start out nice and easy, you know,
agreeing with him, telling him not to worry about
me, he's doing the right thing, and all that stuff.
I might throw in a few little things to shake him
a bit, but nothing big, you know. But then, all of
a sudden," he said slowly, "all of a sudden I might
start to change. Right there in front of him, I
might start to change!"

With this he resumed the pantomime, this time
indicating the nature of his change. Already
slightly slumped at the doorway, as the old man
began to move forward he slumped even further.
As he moved he half turned away from his audience; there was no snap to his step, his progress
appeared to be as painful as it was slow, and his
right foot dragged. As he came closer to them, he
twisted around so that when he stopped he con-

fronted them full-face. He looked, suddenly, very old. His body now began to shake and shake badly. This performance was watched by the three men with the greatest attention, and the attention was on the point of mounting into concern when Daniel miraculously stiffened into his normal upright posture and all shaking ceased. He smiled slightly, and stood there expectantly.

"Oh, very good, Daniel!" Billy cried. "Excellent! A truly magnificent case of the trembles!"

Gottlieb exhaled largely. "Believe me, Daniel," he said, "for one minute there I got a little nervous. A boy looks at his Dad doing that, he could get scared to death."

"Yes yes," Father Feeley agreed. "All the marks of deterioration: first class!"

"It's not bad, at that," Daniel said complacently. "I practiced it a bit, you know, in front of the mirror. That's why I didn't want any of them snooping around, getting wise to what I was doing. It's a damn good stunt, but it's got to be a surprise."

"If it's all the same to you, Daniel, I don't need any more surprises like that," Gottlieb said. "My old friend Artie Glickman dying in a second from a clot, you all crumpled over like a cripple: believe me, it makes me very nervous!"

"Well, that's what it's supposed to do," Daniel said. "It's supposed to make anybody that sees it worried as hell. And don't forget this: you were ready for it. I told you something was coming. But say I sprang it on somebody that was just sitting there, not expecting anything! Well then, maybe we might have some fun!"

"The results can't help but be highly dramatic, my dear man," Billy said. "Unless I miss my guess, restoratives may be needed."

Daniel said, "And then, you know, we don't have to stop with that. There's plenty of other things a man could do. Oh yes. I . . . ah . . . ah . . . ahh . . ."

Without warning, his speech broke off into a choking, gurgling sound; as he uttered it Daniel bent double, then snapped back into an unnaturally stiff, erect position. His face moved as if he had no control over its expression; his tongue popped out and, gasping, he staggered, then collapsed into a chair. He lay there, sprawled out awkwardly, his breathing deep and rasping, one leg jerking spasmodically, his arms flopping bonelessly about. It was altogether an alarming performance and unquestionably it alarmed his audience. Prepared for theatrics, this was something more; they looked at each other and then moved

[149]

a tentative step forward. It was Father Feeley who finally moved briskly to Daniel's side.

"All right, Daniel!" he said peremptorily. "The point is made." There was no answer; the priest said, "Daniel?"

"Oh my God!" Gottlieb cried. "Artie Glickman Number Two!"

In the chair, the harsh breathing and all movement now came to a stop. The three men saw only the slightest rise and fall of the old man's chest; there was no sound. In a moment there was a grunt, a sigh; they watched as slowly Daniel opened his eyes a little and said, very weakly, "Where is he? Where's my personal physician? Why don't I hear from the medical department?" Then his eyes closed again, and as the men looked at one another, suddenly Daniel sat bolt upright in his chair, opened his eyes fully, and spoke to them in his normal voice.

"Well, Billy!" he said. "How about that one? Don't tell me you thought I was a goner, too?"

"My compliments, Daniel," Billy said, recovering rapidly. "My sincere compliments. That was what we might call the performance of a virtuoso! Oh yes! You almost fooled the trained eye with that one, my dear man. You almost fooled *me!*"

"Listen to me, Daniel," Gottlieb said shakily. "With me there was no almost. I admit it: you fooled me. But that kind of fooled I don't want to be. With that kind of fooling you could give a man a condition. So don't show me any more. Whatever you say you can do, all right: I believe it. I'm a convinced person, Daniel!"

"And what about the clergy?" Daniel said, looking at Father Feeley. "By God, you were over here like a shot, I'll say that for you. *Dominus vobiscum* and the big heave-ho to the cemetery lot: was that the idea?"

"More or less, yes yes," Father Feeley said. "The waxen pallor, the ghastly respiration, the twitching: all authentic, extremely so."

"Especially the twitching, my dear man!" Billy said, in full enthusiasm once more. "I don't want to flatter you, Daniel, but those twitches were A-Number-One! You could go to every hospital in the country and you wouldn't find better twitches than those!"

"Well, that's what I told you," Daniel said. "You don't spend fifty years on the stage without picking up a trick or two. Tricks that come in handy every now and again. Like tonight, say. What son could throw his father out when his father's having

fits? Hey, Billy? Specially when they're the kind
of terrible fits I have? What son could be as cruel
as that?"

"What you're talking about there, Daniel, is the
proverbial heart of stone," Billy said. "There's no
danger of that here. Thanks to what we might call
your consummate art."

"A queer business, this mimicry of dying," Father Feeley said. "Children do it all the time, adults
almost never. Understandable, of course. The
closer you are to a thing, the less you want to play
games with it."

"What you say, Father," Gottlieb said urgently,
"it's true. I tell you, Daniel, there's something
about it I don't like. What I don't like is an old
gentleman like you, my own age exactly, lying
flat on his back, kicking his legs up in the air,
going, 'Ah . . . ah . . . ah.'" He shook his head
sadly. "I feel like Father. It's not right. It's not
decent. It could even be dangerous."

"I'd have to disagree with that, my dear man,"
Billy said. "Speaking as a medical man, I have to
disagree with you and Father there. What could
be dangerous about it, with a man like Daniel at
the controls?"

"Right you are, Billy," Daniel said. "There's

damn well nothing dangerous about it at all."

"You've put your finger right on it, my dear man," Billy said. *"There's nothing dangerous at all.* It's just the pessimists, the Gloomy Guses, who always look on the dark side of things. They're always thinking that one day you'll start one of these fake fits and won't be able to pull out of it. They're always thinking of a day you'll be lying there on your back, kicking away and dribbling and turning blue in the face, needing the doctor fast if you're going to last until sunset, but nobody pays a bit of attention to you because they don't know it's the real McCoy caught up with you at last, and not just you having fun! Oh yes, Daniel, they're always thinking about things like that. Good people, yes, but that's the way they think. They're pessimists one and all! They never come around and cheer a man up!"

Daniel gave him a look which was long, exasperated, and baffled. "By God," he said finally, "you've got the damnedest way of cheering people up I ever saw. If you tell a man Happy Birthday he wants to put his head in the oven." He shrugged, and then returned to his main theme. "Anyways, all that's no matter. I don't give a damn about that kind of nonsense. All I want to know is this: do you agree with me? That it'll do the job? With Tom?"

"Put your mind at ease, my dear man," Billy said. "A stunt like that would do the job with a regiment of Toms!"

"Yes, yes, it should be effective, I think," Father Feeley said. "Fairly effective. I don't know the boy well of course. Still, he's probably typical. They're a strange lot. I don't understand them at all. Sometimes they seem scarcely human. Yet we know they're made in the image and likeness of God. There's a mystery for you!"

Daniel said, "But it'll work?"

"Oh yes," Father Feeley said. "I should think so. I should think it might work quite well. And if it doesn't . . . well, there you are. And so forth. In the end, of course, it all means very little."

"Daniel, I'll give you my frank opinion," Gottlieb said. "When I came into this room a while ago, I said something to myself. I said, 'Poor Daniel: he hasn't got a Chinaman's chance. I know young people; they're all like my Sonny.' But now, Daniel, I'll make a confession to you: I changed my mind. Now I say to myself, 'Gottlieb, you spoke too soon. Those fits you saw: they're horrible things. But maybe they'll scare that selfish boy into keeping his good old Dad around!'"

"Good for you, Gottlieb!" Billy said. "It takes a big man to admit he's been wrong. Look at Columbus, Herbert Hoover . . . oh yes, Daniel, I'm all with Gottlieb on that one. I'll go even further than Gottlieb! I'll say you'll not only be around after tonight; you'll be around here for years to come!"

Daniel smiled slightly. "I'll let you in on a little secret, Billy," he said. "I think you're right. I think you're damned right!"

"Yes, yes, you'll be around," Father Feeley said. "For some time to come, perhaps. My private opinion, of course. Anything is possible." He looked around quickly, smoothed his hair back nervously with one hand, and stepped quickly towards Daniel. "I must go," he said. "Goodbye, Daniel. I enjoyed the performance. Very skillful. It took me back to the old days."

"If you don't mind, Father, I'll go along with you," Gottlieb said. He too crossed over to Daniel and said, "Artie Glickman's sister, Daniel. She gets nervous. But many thanks to you and good wishes. It was a pleasure and a privilege."

"I'll make it unanimous, my dear man," Billy said. He went to the bed and picked up his satchel. "Duty calls: I've got to get back to my bladder case before some Official Doctor gets in there and does the usual irreparable damage. Goodbye, Daniel. It was a grand treat. You could have sold tickets."

"No no, this one was on the house," Daniel said. "This one was on me!" He was in great good humor. He shook hands all around, and then walked with his three old friends to the door. Once there, before opening it, he motioned at them with a cautioning gesture. "One second now," he said. He whipped the door open and quickly stepped into the hall, looking in both directions. "It's all right," he said. "I guess some people were minding their own business for a change."

"And after tomorrow, my dear man," Billy said, "we'll all come around to call as usual."

"Ah!" Daniel exclaimed. "By God, I almost forgot the most important part. I tell you when I want you to come. Not after tomorrow; I want you to come tonight! All of you!"

The three men looked at each other; Billy said, "Tonight, my dear man? You want us to come in on the very night you're having the big act with Tom?"

"That's right," Daniel said. "Only not while I'm doing it, of course. I want you to come in afterwards. About nine, say; it'll be all over then. And it'd mean a lot to me to have you around. My doctor, my priest, and my favorite fan: all together backstage at Waltzing Daniel Considine's farewell performance! Will you do it?"

Again the three men looked at each other, and with no hesitation all nodded. Billy said jubilantly, "Right you are, my dear man! We'll be here with bells on! To celebrate the happy occasion!"

"Yes yes," Father Feeley agreed. "Well, goodbye, Daniel." He left the room with a quick little gesture of farewell; it was a curious gesture which might almost have been taken for a benediction.

Gottlieb followed Father Feeley; on the threshold he said, "Goodbye, Daniel. And stay in good health. That way, no matter what happens, at least you've got your health."

Billy was the last to go; as he left he waved and said, "Until tonight, my dear man. Tonight at nine! A rendezvous with us all!"

"Fine, fine, fair enough," Daniel said. "Goodbye again."

Billy closed the door behind him, and Daniel was once more alone. He was obviously pleased with the result of the session; he smiled and rubbed his hands. He spoke aloud, and with great satisfaction.

"Boys oh boys!" he said. "Well well well. It won't be long now. Oh no. It won't be long at all!"

He was looking forward to the encounter; he felt

like a boy. It had been literally years since he had been so excited. He walked quickly to his mirror and stood facing himself, just looking without any particular expression; then he smiled.

"Oh yes!" he said. "Oh yes yes yes yes!"

More soberly, he began to examine himself in detail. He pulled down the lower lid of his left eye and scrutinized the eyeball critically; it was still white, still, fine, still clear. He opened his mouth; he stuck out his tongue and regarded it gravely. He took his pulse as he stood there. Then he stepped back, smoothed his hands over his hair, and looked at himself from head to foot, up and down. He was not displeased with what he saw.

Backing a few steps, he took a deep breath, then abruptly went into the pantomime which had so alarmed his friends. He bent, staggered, limped, and looked older than ever; he collapsed into a chair, and once more the deep and desperate breathing began. The twitches which Billy so admired went on full display. This continued for some moments, after which Daniel got slowly to his feet and returned to his mirror to check on his appearance. He smiled and nodded his head.

"Oh yes," he said again. "We'll see about that! We will, we will!"

This finished, he looked about him as if he were not quite sure what came next. His eyes stopped at the record player on the table; he went over to it, picked the record off, looked at it, then replaced it. He turned up the volume and waited; soon, fading in, came the music of his theme song, and as it did, old Daniel, alone in his room, began to dance, singing softly but happily as he did so:

I'll tell you who's a friend of mine —
He's Waltzing Daniel Considine!
Dum dee, dum dee, dum dum dee dum
Dum dum dee dum di dum
Dum dum dee di dee, dee dum dum dee di
Dum dum dee di dee, dum dum dee di. . . .

And as he danced he reflected that it would be three hours, now, before his son came, before his act began. Eager, impatient, he could hardly wait for the moment. He wished that it were *now. . . .*

six

THE law office had a tradition of prompt arrival and departure — in at nine, out at five — but tonight, when the others had gone, Tom stayed on. He did not stay long; after perhaps half an hour the pointlessness, even the ludicrousness, of such postponement struck him so forcibly that he jumped up, left the office, and set out for home. For most of the way he walked with a quick decisive step.

His talk with his father was not to take place until after dinner. He was not, now, especially hungry; he was almost grateful, therefore, for the light and barely edible meal which the maid had left for him in the kitchen. It was her night out; she had gone by the time he arrived, and so he ate at the kitchen table, alone in the house with his father. As he ate he heard the occasional sounds of movement upstairs; he tried his old morning game of guessing what his father was about, but with no more success than ever. He ate quickly and without really tasting his food; now and then he looked at his watch, anticipating, not the meeting to come, but the moment when it would be over. Unlike his father, he did not at all look forward to the meeting itself; he had none of the old man's joy of combat. He could not for the life of him imagine this last face-to-face talk as being anything but unpleasant — even supposing there were no hitches, that all went unexpectedly well — and he did not like unpleasantness. Particularly when the unpleasantness was a family matter, when it involved someone who was, after all, his father. . . .

"You kill me," Jack Pomeroy had said to him, one day when the subject of Daniel had come up. "You're a puddle of sentiment. You can't even mention your father without thinking that he should be Dear Old Dad. You start wondering about duties and obligations — even though he never gave a damn about his. You start to feel guilty because you don't feel what you think you're supposed to feel. You know what your trouble is? You have no experience: you've never thrown your father out before. Of course I haven't mine, either, but he threw *me* out, and the net effect was the same.

We've both done very well ever since. I've never felt better and neither has he. You're just reversing the process, that's all."

Tom had not paid much attention to this; he considered Jack a poor counsel on filial responsibilities. Still, he sometimes envied him his clear-cut approach to his father: it was one of plain, undeviating dislike. Probably with good reason, Tom thought; he had seen enough of old Mr. Pomeroy in the office to imagine what he had been like as a parent. And he remembered Jack, at school, attempting to escape from his father's far-reaching and ruthless scrutiny.

Whereas with Tom there had been no scrutiny at all. It had not been welcome, this freedom; he had been able to distinguish, quite early, between the indulgent hand and simple neglect. Neglect of him and, of course, neglect of his mother. Tom had been close to his mother; she had seldom spoken to him of his father, but he had always sensed her extreme bitterness — a bitterness which seemed to have been fed, rather than weakened, by Daniel's rare overnight returns to his home. She had died twenty years ago, apparently without forgiving her husband. Daniel had come home for the funeral, arriving just in time for Mass. He had

spoken of an interrupted engagement; he had ex-
pressed sorrow quickly; he had remained dry-eyed;
he had talked briefly and uneasily to his son; four
hours later, he was gone. And after that Tom had
not seen him for twenty years.

He had not missed him. He had come to feel for
this remote parent almost nothing at all. All the
emotions he had once felt for his father faded in
time as Tom grew older and as, finally, Daniel disappeared from view. It was truly out of sight, out of
mind: in the long and all but incredible interval
of the old man's absence, his son seldom thought
of him. Never knowing him well, and now not
knowing him at all, he thought of him only occasionally, tangentially, impersonally, and after his
own marriage even these thoughts grew fewer.
Sometimes — usually when he was in bed, waiting
to go to sleep, or when he was in the office and not
occupied — he might feel a twitch, a pull from the
past, and then he would recall his father for an
instant in a sudden, stronger, more disturbing
light, but this did not happen often, and on the
whole, for all practical purposes, Tom could be
said to have forgotten his father.

Until of course the reappearance: the unex-
pected apparition on the doorstep at midnight.

This had made a difference to Tom — a greater difference than he had at first realized. Now, for the first time as an adult, he could no longer regard Daniel as an abstraction; for the first time in his life he had come to some sort of grips with the living, breathing person who was his father. The new experience had been a confusing one. At first startled by the old man's arrival, then curious about him, Tom had grown to be absorbed, and for the past year his mind had been filled with his father. Memories, long forgotten or subdued, came back, all of them; for the most part they were not pleasant memories. Against these he discovered that Daniel had a charm he had not suspected, and there had been a time when Daniel had slowly begun to creep up on him, when he found himself looking at his father and, in spite of everything, including himself, grudgingly liking him, and wondering if perhaps the old judgments might not have been too harsh, and remembering two or three occasions on which he had behaved badly towards the old man, and thinking that however his father had been in the past, it was quite possible that age had brought change. . . .

These speculations had not lasted. As Daniel had stayed on, his charm had worn thin; also, his design had become clearer. Tom saw it, and also saw the old man in relation to his wife; gradually he had summed up his softer thoughts as wishful thinking, and he knew that his father would have to go. He had made the decision months ago; now that the time at last had come to execute it, he was unhappy.

Sitting at the kitchen table, he went over the points once more. He knew that what he was doing was right. He knew that any other course was impossible: that Daniel, in this house much longer, would produce disaster. To keep him would not be kind; it would be ruinous. He knew that — and he knew, too, that while the old man was being sent off against his will, he was not being sent off to hardship or discomfort: the accommodations at the Smiling Valley were good, ample, even plush; the institution was the best of its kind. And finally, he told himself, there was no question of injustice, of ingratitude: certainly all debts to his father, even presuming they had existed, had been paid off long ago. So then, he was not behaving badly, he had no grounds for self-reproach, for uneasiness. . . .

And yet he was uneasy. He was uneasy precisely because, in a few minutes, and for the first time,

he would have his father at his mercy. The old
positions of authority were now reversed: it was
now Tom who was calling the tune; his father
could do nothing but obey. It was as simple as that.
Tom did not share his wife's almost superstitious
regard for his father's cunning, his resourceful-
ness. He knew that Daniel was a very tricky man,
and that now he would indeed pull out all the
stops, but — what were those stops? And, once
pulled — what then? Tom did not know what
angle his father would take; he could not see that
it would make any great difference. For his part,
he had decided to say very little, to let his father
say what he would until, at last, he had talked himself out. And that would be that. He could not
imagine the old man's saying or doing anything
which would cancel or even postpone his departure. Tom had little conceit; he knew that in many
ways his father was far more adroit than he; he
also knew that here, tonight, mere adroitness would
not count. This talk between his father and himself was not a competition of abilities. It was not
a competition at all. It was a confrontation in
which, as he had said to his wife, Tom held all
the cards. His father had none. In a word, he was
helpless.

It was this helplessness of his father which, more than anything else, troubled Tom. He felt that it was somehow wrong that he should even be in such a position in relation to his father: a position where his father might have to *beg* from him. And as he thought of this — the possibility of Daniel's begging him for a stay — he winced and closed his eyes and again told himself that this was not the way it should be at all. . . .

Nevertheless, this was the way it was. He pushed his plate away and rose from the kitchen table. He stood by the table for one last hesitating moment; then, quickly, he left the kitchen and began to walk up the back stairway, which would take him almost directly to his father's room.

seven

WHEN Tom went up to his father's room at last, it was nearly eight o'clock. Daniel had been expecting him for some time. Since his guests had left that afternoon, the old man had been preparing himself for the evening — and preparing not only himself, but his setting as well. He considered this to be of the greatest importance, for he had the old actor's feeling for the proper backdrop. Now, everything that was his own in the room had been packed, and his two old suitcases, with their leather binding straps around them, stood on the floor at the foot of his bed. Next to the suitcases were three large cardboard cartons; secured with rope, they contained his scrapbooks. On top of these he had placed his record player; it was closed and ready to go. Propped up in the front of the pile was the WALTZ-ING DANIEL CONSIDINE poster which had been removed from its dominant position on the wall. Everything was ready for departure, and the result was that the room, although still completely furnished, now had a barrenness which it did not have before. This was an effect which Daniel had thought desirable, and which he had worked painstakingly to achieve.

Since seven o'clock he had been waiting for his son. He knew he was in the house; he had heard him come in. But he had not come up and Daniel, who had been sitting in his chair, waiting, was growing impatient. His careful plans had been completed, he was ready, he ached to begin. Only his son was missing and Daniel, sitting and waiting, glanced often and with increasing irritation at his watch.

Yet he was not idle; he did not stay in his chair. A perfectionist, he got up now and then to improve upon his scene. Shortly before eight an idea occurred to him; he got up quickly, went over to his suitcases, opened one and closed it again, but this time so that the toe of one sock was hanging out. The little touch of pathos pleased him; he went back to his chair nodding his satisfaction.

He had been waiting only a minute or so more when he lifted his head, hearing footsteps. A matter of seconds later, and the knock came. And now, for the first and only time, he showed some sign of tension, of nervousness, for his hands shot out and tightly gripped the arms of his chair. But he relaxed almost immediately, exhaled deeply, and sat back, motionless, to wait for the knock to sound again. It did, and with it came Tom's voice saying, "Dad?"

It was the call he had heard every night for the past month; this time he answered. "Hello, Tom," he said. "I'll be right with you."

But he did not go directly to the door. Instead, he rose and went to the exact center of the room, where, turning, he carefully took in every detail of his surroundings. The inspection completed, he walked over to his mirror for the last time this day, and it was here, now, that all preparation came to an end, and his performance began. He started to sag, slowly, into an older, sadder, more abject figure, critically regarding himself all the while. When he was satisfied that the proper stage had been reached — for he did not want, at this point, to go too far — he gave a curt, businesslike nod, and walked to the door with a shuffling step. At the door he paused; then, quickly, he opened it.

For just the briefest of instants, as the door

snapped open and he caught his first glimpse of his father, Tom was startled and showed it. Then, remembering, he controlled himself, and looked at his father with no particular expression on his face. He said only, "Hi."

"Well, Tom," Daniel said, smiling and putting out his hand. "It's good to see you again. Oh yes. Come in, come in. Don't stand here at the door like a stranger."

Tom shook his father's hand, and as he dropped it he entered the room, looking about him, observing the bags on the floor, the new bleakness. He made no comment.

"Over there, Tom," Daniel said, pointing. "Take a load off your feet. Sit down in that comfortable chair. We can at least say what we have to say to each other sitting down. Even if it's only goodbye."

Tom, still saying nothing, walked to the chair indicated, his back to his father. Daniel did not take his eyes off him. Silently, he closed the door, watching his son: his stare was tough, calculating, and grim. He stared in this way until Tom, turning to sit down, faced him once more; the toughness instantly left the old man's face and he began to move forward to a chair directly opposite Tom. He walked with the slow and slightly shuffling step he had adopted for the occasion. Tom watched him closely, but on his face there was no emotion. As Daniel came close to him, he said, "Hurt your foot?"

"What?" Daniel said, easing himself into the chair with a sigh. "Foot, Tom? Oh. No no, nothing like that. I suppose it's more a case of the old parts wearing out. I don't get any younger, you know."

Tom said, "None of us do that, Dad."

"No," said Daniel. The spirit of this response left a good deal to be desired, but he continued without breaking stride. "That's true enough, Tom: none of us get any younger. Still, I notice it more than most, I s'pose. On account of my age. And on account of the legs. It's the legs that always counted with me." He looked down with great fondness at his legs. "I don't know how many thousands of miles I put on these legs, Tom. They've gone through a hell of a lot. Fifty years of dancing. And never a single cramp. How's that for a record? By God, I might put that on my tombstone: *Fifty years of dancing, and never a single cramp.* That's because I always took care of them. I always kept the legs in grand shape. Oh yes, Tom, I know all about legs. When it comes to legs, it takes a dancer to give you the real lowdown!"

He said this with a triumphant combativeness, as if he expected and invited rebuttal, but Tom merely nodded. There was a pause; the subject of legs seemed to have gone as far as it could go. Both men sat looking at each other; both seemed to be waiting for something. There was a tension, growing greater; it was Daniel who spoke first.

"By God, Tom," he said, "you'll never wear yourself out talking, will you? But that's all right, because you're a hell of a listener. I watched you there, looking at me while I was talking, not missing a trick, and do you know what I said to myself? I said, 'By God, there's a man that'd be great stuff in a courtroom. The way he listens, they'd get nothing past him. There's a man that should of been a lawyer!' I swear to God that's what I said to myself, Tom. And then all of a sudden I remembered, and I said, 'What the hell am I talking about? He *is* a lawyer! And who should know that better than me, the one that put him through law school?' Would you believe it, Tom? That I said a thing like that to myself? I must be getting old!"

Tom nodded again, but he still did not speak. He thought he saw, clearly enough, the direction the talk was about to take; he was resolved to let it go on without interruption. Daniel, who might have

welcomed a reply, nevertheless moved right along
without one, speaking now with a rapid, sudden
expansiveness.

"But what are we talking about all that for?" he
cried, throwing his hands apart. "That's the worst
of being an old man: you go back through all the
years, you know, and think of all the things you
said, and all the things you did for people. And it's
all in the past, isn't that right? Who the hell wants
to hear anything about that stuff? We're not here
to talk about what happened *then*. No. Not by a
damn sight. What we want to talk about is what
happens *now*. To you and the wife. And to me.
Isn't that about the size of it, Tom?"

Tom said, "That's about the size of it, Dad."

"By God, Tom," Daniel said, "you keep that up
and they'll pull you in for running off at the mouth.
A regular chatterbox! But anyways, joking to one
side, in the last month I've been up here alone I've
been doing a lot of thinking, you know, the way a
man does. About a lot of things. About going out to
the Smiling Valley, for instance. By God, I thought
I'd done about everything a man could do in my
life, but this'll be a new one on me, all right! Waltzing Daniel Considine in an Old Man's Home! You
know what some people would say about that,

Tom? They'd say it was a damn bad shake. But
I'll tell you a little secret: I don't know that it is.
No, now that I've thought it all over, I don't know
that it is at all. You've made all the arrangements,
have you? The way you said you would?"

Resignation? A trouble-free passage? In spite of
his experience, Tom felt a stab of optimism, but
then, remembering, he said cautiously, "Everything's all set, Dad."

"Good, good!" Daniel said enthusiastically.
"You're a man of your word, Tom: I'm glad to
see that. I suppose that's the way the law trains a
man: follow through. Well, anyways, I don't feel
so bad about going out there, now I know everything's taken care of. Have you been out there
yourself to see the room they're giving me, Tom?
Is it a nice room? It's nice and big, I hope?"

"It's a very nice room, Dad."

"I know that, Tom," Daniel said. "Oh yes, I knew
it would be nice. I knew it would be the best. After
all, fair is fair. I gave you the very best, back there
when I put you through all those good schools, you
give me the very best today. Isn't that right, Tom?"

Resignation — but with reproach. Tom made no
answer; Daniel smiled encouragingly at him and
continued.

"So there we are," he said. "By the way, don't worry about me getting out there. I know you and the wife would take me out, but Billy Ryan, my doctor, is coming in to do it. Billy and a couple more of my old pals. Oh yes, they'll be in tonight to see me off in style."

This surprised Tom; he said, "Tonight: that's fast work."

"Is it, Tom?" Daniel said. "Well, I'm a fast worker. When I have to be, you know."

"I don't think you have to be that fast, do you? The middle of the night: that's not necessary. You know that."

"Do I, Tom?" Daniel said. "Well, maybe I do. And maybe I don't. Anyways, I'm going. You can see I'm all packed." He waved around, indicating the room stripped of all his possessions; he pointed to the suitcases on the floor. Tom followed his hand, but said nothing.

"So you could say, I suppose," Daniel said, "that I'm ready and waiting. Well, not waiting, exactly, but there it is and we can't change what's to be, can we? Oh no, Tom, I tell you I thought it all over while I was up here by myself. I don't say I didn't feel bad at first. You can understand that, Tom. Being a lawyer and all. If a man gets a kick in the

[176]

arse, specially when he doesn't expect it, he feels it. Even if the feller that kicks him tells him it's really a birthday present after all. But I've got all over that. Now I see you did what you had to do, you and the wife. You're young people, you've got your own lives to live, it's all ahead of you. And I've lived most of mine, it's all behind me. So it's only fair that I get out and let you alone. Anyways, that's one way to look at it. Isn't that right, Tom?"

He said carefully, "That's one way, Dad."

"Of course there's another way to look at it, too," Daniel said. "What I mean is this, Tom. I say I'll go, but when you come right down to it, what the hell else could I say? That I *won't* go? I'm an old man: what can I do *but* go, if you want me to? You could say I was made to, whether I wanted to or not. Isn't that right, Tom? Isn't that a good way to look at it?"

To this Tom made no answer; he was watching his father. Daniel returned his look, nodding cheerfully, and went on talking.

"But why the hell should you answer that one? There's no need to, Tom: I know what your answer would be. That you don't like to look at it that way. And I don't blame you, Tom. I don't think it's a good way to look at it, either. And d'ye know why?

Because it's silly. It makes me out to be helpless, and I'm not. Not by a long shot. I'm an old man, but an old man with a few brains in his head can still do a thing or two if he's in a tight spot. For instance, there was this television thing. I don't think I told you about that, Tom. No, I guess I didn't. Well, I'll tell you now: you'll get a kick out of it. You've got the sense of humor for this one."

He gave Tom an encouraging smile; Tom looked back at him noncommittally. He wondered: What now?

"You see," Daniel explained, "this old feller, an old pal of mine, came in to see me the other afternoon. Most of the time he just sits home, watching the television. I don't watch it myself: it's nothing but cowboys and kids' games. But anyways, he watches it, and he was telling me about a show they have on every week with old people on it. Not just ordinary old people, you know, but old people that used to be famous or popular years back. It's called 'Where Are They Today?' or something like that. Well, they bring on the old people and talk to them and their pals, and find out where they are now and what they're doing. Did you ever see that show, Tom?"

Tom said, "Once or twice, Dad."

"Once or twice," Daniel repeated. "And tell me this, Tom: is it a poor kind of show, would you say?"

"Very poor."

"Very poor!" Daniel, for some reason, seemed delighted. "By God, you know, I thought it sounded like one! But they tell me a hell of a lot of people watch it. And this old feller that came in to see me was telling me all about it and all of a sudden he said, 'You know who should be on that show, Daniel? *You* should!' 'The hell with that,' I said, 'I'm retired.' 'All the better,' he said. 'You're just the kind of a man they want. All over the country there's loads of people used to go to the theater to see Waltzing Daniel Considine, and they'd love to see him again and know how he is today!' Well by God, Tom, what a crazy idea that was! Hey? Imagine a thing like that! I mean, there I'd be, up on some stage, with a camera on me, and some jackass of a radio announcer smiling his fake smile and asking me all sorts of questions. About myself. And about you and the wife too, of course. 'Well now, Mr. Considine, after fifty years of dancing all over the world, and bringing so much happiness to so many people, you must be a happy man yourself to be back in your home at last, living with your only boy and his wife?' 'Well, yes, I was, only that's not quite the way it is now. I'm not there any more, you know.' 'Not there any more! Well well well! We were told you were right where you always wanted to be: back with your family at last.' 'Yes, that's right: that's what I wanted. But it didn't work out that way. Young people these days like to have things to themselves, so I had to go.' 'Go! Oh my my! That must be terrible for you, Mr. Considine, at your age. And where did you have to go to?' 'Oh, it's not too bad, I suppose. I've got a nice enough little room in the Old Man's Home where they put me. It's small, you know, but I've got a nice view of the street and the little cemetery in the back. So I don't complain. It's not what I counted on, but I don't blame anybody. They probably did what they thought was right. It's not for me to judge.'" He stopped and looked at his son with wide and innocent eyes. "By God, Tom," he said, "wouldn't that be the damnedest thing, though! All that stuff going out all over the country! And maybe right here in the city lots of people you know or do business with would see it! By God, imagine what they'd make out of a thing like that! And imagine me *doing* a thing like that! I wonder can you imagine that, Tom?"

It was blackmail; his father had decided to be tough rather than tearful; Tom almost sighed his relief. The particular threat did not bother him. The office had as one of its clients a large television station, and Tom had become fairly familiar with the principles and techniques of that industry; he thought it likely that his father's plan would remain just that. And so he said nothing, but stared thoughtfully at his father; Daniel looked at him steadily, appraisingly, and for just a second his smile disappeared entirely. Then, suddenly, it returned, and the old man went on talking.

"The cat's got your tongue, Tom, hey? Well, never mind, I know what you mean: you *can't* imagine it. You can't imagine your old Dad doing a thing like that to you. And you're right, Tom. Oh yes, you're right. But are you right for the right reasons? I don't think you are, Tom. I can look right in your eyes and see that lawyer's mind working away in back there. I know damn well what you're thinking. You're thinking the only reason I don't do it is because I can't get on the show, that they only pick one out of every two hundred or so that try to get on. Well, you're wrong there, Tom. And you're wrong too if you think I don't go on because I found out that they do the whole thing on film

[181]

beforehand so's they can cut out parts that might get them sued or in trouble. A man can't be sure that even a damn word he says will finally get out on the air. But if you think I'm thinking like that, Tom, you're wrong and wrong all the way. No, the real reason I don't go on that show is this: *there's some things a decent man doesn't do to his own flesh and blood.* No matter what they do to him. *That's* why I don't go on that show. You don't believe that, do you, Tom?"

Tom was suddenly tired of silence. He felt an urge to speak, to stop what was essentially a monologue which, for all he knew, might very well go on all night. Moreover, he felt that he had something to say to his father, something it was important for the old man to understand. He leaned forward in his chair and said, "Dad. Look: I —"

But Daniel cut in on him fast. "Don't apologize," he said, waving magnanimously. "No no, that's not necessary. I forgive you, there's no need to say you're sorry. But is that what you were going to say, Tom? Did I interrupt you there? You looked like you were all set to start out on a little speech."

But the urge to speak, to talk frankly to his father, to bring matters to a head more quickly had passed as swiftly as it had come. He realized that

he could not make his father understand; he realized too that it was easier — and quicker — in the
long run to let his father set his own pace. With a
movement of his hand he indicated that the floor
was still Daniel's.

"Well, all right," Daniel said. "I just didn't want
to butt in. Even if I could. By God, you know, Tom,
it's not the easiest thing in the world to put the
brakes on a nonstop talker like you. Isn't that right,
Tom?" He smiled again, encouraging comment;
then, without waiting for it, he continued more
seriously. "But all joking aside, I wouldn't go near
a show like that. I retired from all that stuff long
ago, anyways. They won't get Waltzing Daniel
Considine out on a stage again. Or on television,
either. No, it's all over now, and when a thing is
over, it's over. Finished and done. It's just like living in the house here. I had a good time, I don't say
I didn't, but it's over. And so I say what I said before: All right. I'll go, and I'll go with no hard feeling. Is that fair, Tom?"

"That's fair, Dad," Tom said. "That's very fair."

"So that I suppose you could say," Daniel said,
"that this is our last night together. A boy and his
Dad. They used to put that kind of stuff on magazine covers. D'ye think we'd be any good for that,

Tom? Could they make a nice magazine cover out of the both of us, do you suppose? Maybe they could give us a fishpole to hold? Or a puppy? Or would we have to have something more than that?"

Tom said suddenly, "Would you believe it if I told you something? I know how you feel, but would you believe it if I told you this wasn't the greatest moment in my life, either?"

"It hurts you more than it does me: is that it, Tom?"

"No," he said, with irritation. "No, I didn't say that. And I didn't mean it. All I said was —"

"I heard what you said, Tom," Daniel said, interrupting again. "And I thank you. But you don't have to say anything more. You go your way and I'll go mine. I'll be all right, don't worry about that. I've always been able to take good care of myself. I've always had to. I didn't have anyone to take care of all my bills and bring me up and see to it that I was educated with the finest in the country. No, I did it all by myself, and that's the way I can do it still!" He rose from his chair, still talking, and with each word his voice seemed to grow louder, more excited.

"Oh yes!" he cried. "Old as I am, sick as I am, I

can still get out of here and show you all a thing or two! I'm not done yet, not by a long shot! I can still . . . still. . . ."

And the words died off in his mouth; he seemed to struggle to force them out, then quit. The words were succeeded by a series of gasps and gurgles. At last, Daniel was going into the act for which he had so carefully prepared. He staggered, pointing to his mouth; his eyes were unnaturally wide; he groped his way over towards his bed. Reaching this he collapsed, moaning and writhing. This continued for some seconds and then, abruptly, the motion stopped and Daniel lay still. His face was absolutely immobile, and his eyes were now closed tight. One leg jerked spasmodically; his breathing was hoarse, deep, grating. Altogether, it was fully as alarming as the rehearsal that afternoon, but now there was one significant difference. For where the audience that afternoon had viewed his performance with attention and then the deepest concern, Tom now showed neither. In fact, after jerking his head up at the first groans and gasps and looking sharply at his father, he seemed to lose interest entirely. Not only did he watch without any show of emotion when Daniel staggered to his bed, but during the latter part of the turbulent exhibition he did not even look at his father. Instead, he rose, turned, and walked over to the window. Here he stood looking out into the evening, while Daniel went through his concluding maneuvers. Finally Daniel stopped entirely; his breathing grew quieter, more subdued; he lay on his bed, not moving. Both men waited, and it was Tom, still staring out the window, who spoke first.

"It's no use, Dad," he said wearily. "It won't wash."

Daniel said weakly, "Tom . . . Tom . . ."

"No no no," Tom said sharply. "Cut it out. It's another game. And this one I'm not playing."

Daniel did not respond; he said faintly, "Agh . . . agh . . . agh . . ."

Tom shook his head. "Fake, Dad," he said. "Fake, fake, fake. It's the very last thing you should be faking about, but you're doing it anyway, aren't you?" Now he swung around to face his father, and for the first time there was a touch of pain in his voice. "Cut it out, Dad. Please. It's humiliating. Degrading. Because I know what you're doing, and you know that I know, don't you?"

There was a silence. Tom did not move, but stood staring at his father as if trying to will him to speech. For a moment Daniel did nothing; even his gasping had ceased. Then, slowly, he raised himself on one elbow and looked across at his son. When he spoke his voice was normal in volume, but packed with bitterness.

"*You know,*" he said. "You know a hell of a lot, don't you? Are you proud of yourself, Tom? You must be!"

"Proud," Tom repeated. "Proud because I could watch my father dive all around the room in a deathbed act, and know the whole thing was a fraud? You have a funny idea of pride, Dad."

"Sneaking around outside a man's door," Daniel said, "spying on what he's doing, listening to what he says to his friends! Oh yes, that's something to be proud of, all right!"

Tom said, wearily again, "Nobody sneaked, nobody spied. That wasn't how I knew. I just knew, that's all. I just took one look at you, and I *knew.*"

Slowly, Daniel got up from the bed. When he spoke he seemed to address the room rather than his son. "I'm getting out of this house," he said. "In five minutes."

There was no reaction to this. Tom had turned away from Daniel again, and once more faced the window.

"In five minutes from now," Daniel said, still

[187]

speaking to the room, "they can run all over the house, the two of them, all by themselves at last. They can go into every room and into all the closets and look under all the beds and chairs and couches, and they won't see a soul but themselves, and they won't hear a voice but their own. And then they can stand belly to belly and hold each other tight and smile into each other's eyes and whisper, 'We did it! It's all over now, and we've got it all to ourselves. We don't have to share anything with anybody now, because we did it. Aren't we smart, the two of us? Aren't we grand? Take a look at us, and give us a medal while you're at it! Because do you know what we just did? We just beat a sick old man!' "

He stopped, breathing heavily; Tom, still facing the window, gripped the sill with his hands tightly.

"Yes," Daniel said, "that's what they'll say. And they can say it in five minutes. Because in five minutes I'll be out of here, and I'll be out of here forever!"

Tom, still with his back to his father, and still gripping the windowsill, said in a controlled voice, "You do just as you please, Dad."

There was another silence. Daniel stood staring at his son's back. Finally he said, "By God, what a son! Your father means a lot to you, doesn't he?"

"Ah, well!" Tom said. He turned now to face his father; he spoke to him in a flat, deliberate voice. "How about putting that another way? How about saying that my father means as much to me as his son ever did to him? I think that's fair."

"How the hell do you know what you mean to me?" Daniel said loudly. "You never say more than ten words in a row, and no matter how much I talked to you I couldn't get through to you to tell you anything!"

"It's a little late in the day for conversation, isn't it?" Tom said.

"Oho!" Daniel cried. "You're coming to life now, are you? Now you've got what you want, you'll talk a mile a minute, is that it?"

"No," Tom said. He knew that against his plan, against his wishes, possibly against his best interest, he was being drawn into argument with his father. But he was conscious now of a pressure to talk, a pressure of so many things inside him that had never been said, and that should be said. He said, "I said it's a little late for conversation, remember? I'm forty-four years old, Dad. From the time I was born until I was more than twenty, I saw you . . . how often? Twice a year? Three

times in a really big year? And then for the next
twenty years I never saw you at all. So I'm sorry
you can't get through to me, but you don't get A-
for-effort. It hasn't been exactly a lifelong try."

"Cold, Tom," Daniel said. "You're cold. Cold as
the moon. You're a cold boy and you always were.
I knew it the very first time I laid eyes on you. It
was in the hospital right after you were born. I remember I went in and they took me up and showed
you to me; you were lying there in some fancy kind
of a crib — a bassinet, I think they called it. I
looked down at you, and I said, 'Hello, Sonny.' All
I knew about you was you were a boy: you were
too little to even have a name yet. So I said, 'Hello
Sonny. I'm your Dad.' And what did you do? I'll tell
you what you did, Tom: you gave me a smile.
Small as you were, you gave me a smile. But Tom:
d'ye know what kind of a smile?"

Tom said, "I'll make a guess: a cold smile."

"Right!" Daniel cried. "A cold smile! *It was the
coldest smile I ever saw on a child.* Even the nurse
noticed it. 'Why, Mr. Considine,' she said to me,
'we very seldom get babies in here that smile like
that!' I never told you that before, did I, Tom?
Does it make you think a little? A baby, not one
week old, giving cold smiles to his father!"

"You've got a great memory, Dad," Tom said. "How are you on current events? For example, do you remember a man standing here on the front porch a year ago, saying, 'I've just dropped by to say hello. I wanted to see my son once more, and to meet his wife as well. No no, I'm on my way through town, I can't stay more than a minute!' Remember that, Dad? A pretty good minute, wasn't it?"

"Cold cold cold!" Daniel said loudly. "Cold baby, cold man: that's the way it always works out. You could give a boy like that the stars, and it's no more to him than if you handed him a Hershey bar. He won't appreciate it, and he damn well won't thank you for it. No no, cold all the way through: cold head, cold heart, cold bones!"

"Look," Tom said sharply. "If it comes to that, what —" But he did not continue; he stopped short, as if suddenly warned that what he was doing now was precisely what he had sworn not to do. He stared at his father, then slowly the challenge went out of his eyes, and he shrugged. In a quieter voice, one intended to pacify, he said, "I'm sorry. This is just bickering. And I don't want to bicker with you, Dad."

But either Daniel did not hear him, or he did not wish to be pacified. "Oh yes!" he said, persisting.

"And if you give a boy like that good schools, fine clothes, and all the spending money he can use — what are you? I'll tell you what you are: you're a damned fool! Gottlieb was right: give them everything, and what you'll get back for it is a cold eye and a set of directions to the next bus out of town!"

Irritation flashed; his father was hard on good resolutions. He said impatiently, "Look, what is all this, anyway? We're back in Fairyland again with The Legend of the Good Provider. Once upon a time there was a little boy who was sent to private schools, college and law school. He had cash in his pockets, and his pants were better than corduroy. All right: let's accept that. And having accepted it — what about it?"

"What *about* it?" Daniel said, incredulous. "What *about* it?"

"Yes, exactly," Tom said. "What about it?" Almost jubilantly, he knew his silence was over. Suddenly something in him had given way; he felt as he had never felt before. All the memories of everything old Daniel had done now seemed to come in on him, all together but at the same time with great individual clarity, and he wanted nothing more than to face his father with each of them, to hold them up to him, to shake them before his face, to show him what he was, to — in a sense —

pay him back. Rarely angry, he was angry now;
ordinarily quiet, the words now could not come
fast enough. He said, his voice trembling a little,
"You say we never talk: well, let's talk now. Let's
talk a little cold turkey. No matter what you gave
me, you got out of it cheap. Apart from a certain
amount of money, you didn't go to bat with a single responsibility all along the line. You ducked
them all. You're a great ducker, Dad. You took the
easy way out: you paid the bills and stayed away."

Daniel said, "I never claimed I was a family
man in the ordinary way —"

"Which means what?" Tom said. "That you were
one in some *extra*ordinary way? Cut it out, Dad.
This whole thing is right out of the funny papers.
You talk as if you'd just been voted Father of the
Year. You seem to think that some mighty injustice
is being done you. Why? I don't get it. I really don't.
You turn up here after twenty years of nonexist-
ence as far as I was concerned, and damned little
existence before that. But up you turn, and in you
come. For how long? Overnight? A week? A
month? No, a *year.* One full, solid year. Well, in
my book, that's not a bad run. Especially when all
you were supposed to do in the first place was
come in and take a bow!"

"Who the hell are you, the manager of the Palace?" Daniel said angrily. "What right have you got to tell me what I'm supposed to do or what I'm not supposed to do?"

"All the right in the world, when what you're not supposed to be doing you *are* doing in my house. In Ellen's house."

"Oho!" Daniel crowed. "There we have it! In Ellen's house! I knew we'd get down to business before long. You're a cold boy, Tom, but you're a weak one. You wouldn't do all this by yourself. No, it's the wife that's calling the tune on this one, isn't that right, Tom? How's she doing it, I wonder? Does she say, 'Get him out of here by half-past midnight at the latest, or I'll put on my pouty face and be mad at you'? Does she scare you by saying things like that to you, Tom?"

"Do you want to know exactly what she does say, Dad?" Tom said. "She says that it's a nice house we have here, but a small one, and that in the last year it's been getting smaller by the day. She says that all of a sudden she's become a little bit tired of never being able to be *alone* in her house any more during the day, or of never being sure that she can talk privately and without interruption to her husband at night. She says that among other things she finds it no pleasure to provide room service,

[194]

maid service, a telephone answering service, and special foods for someone who seems to regard it as increasingly his right to receive them, and who seldom if ever thanks her for them. She says she's not fond of total strangers under any circumstances, and she's much less fond of them when they come trooping into her home at all hours and seem to regard it as a kind of clubhouse for the old pals of Waltzing Daniel Considine. And finally, Dad, she has a word to say about you. She says that about a year ago you made a big decision: you decided to change your act. After working solo all your life, you came up with a brand new routine: Waltzing Daniel Considine and His Two Stooges. Well, it was a great act while it lasted, Dad, but it's all over now. *Kaput.* The two stooges are dealing themselves out."

"By God," Daniel said, "it's what I said from the beginning: any time there's trouble, the nigger in the woodpile is always a woman!"

"Not in this woodpile, Dad," Tom said. "This nigger's all boy: the girl just came in to second the motion. Everything Ellen said, I said first, and a little bit more besides. But it's all over now. We've had it; we're done. You spread yourself all over our lives, Dad, and you did it before we even realized what was happening. Which doesn't say much for us, does it? You just kept drifting in a little more every day, and we didn't even have the brains to put up a snow fence. So in the end what did we have on our hands but the Japanese gardener all over again. You remember that story, don't you? You ought to. The Japanese gardener comes in in the beginning to nurse a few tulips along, and the next thing you know he's saying, 'So sorry: this my garden now.' Well, it's as simple as this, Dad: we want our garden back."

"I thank God I had only the one son," Daniel said. "Two like you would of been more than a man could stand!"

"Wrong," Tom said. "If you'd had two sons, you know what you'd have done? You'd have broken away twice as fast, and come home half as often. Look: don't you really know what's gumming up the works? I'll tell you if you don't. It's the fact that in spite of everything you still think of yourself as a father. Let me clear this up for you. In this city today there are twenty men, all about your age, who have no family ties with me, who have never given me a cent, who had no special reason and certainly no obligation to help me or even to like me. And yet from every one of them I've gotten more kindness, advice, assistance, and just plain human consideration than I've ever gotten from you — and to every one of them I feel closer, infinitely closer, than I do to you. Now this is a fact, Dad: a simple fact. Does it suggest anything to you?"

"You're damned right it does!" Daniel snapped. "It suggests to me that I had the bad luck to wind up with the coldest, most unnatural son ever born this side of the Rocky Mountains!"

"Does it?" Tom said. "I'll tell you what it suggests to me. It suggests that if you'd been any kind of father at all — and I mean *any* kind: even one of those pathetic little half-assed, skirt-chasing drunks who nevertheless manage to get home a couple of nights a week to say hello or maybe stick on a Band-Aid if somebody gets cut — even if you'd been one of those I don't think I could say what I did. But I can say it. And I can mean it. And I do mean it. And that's what makes the difference, Dad. That's what makes all the difference!"

Once more there was a silence, a silence pulled so tight that it almost twanged. The two men confronted each other, standing very close; they had come forward bit by bit as they talked so that now they were nearly touching. Daniel, from an inch away, glared at his son; Tom met the look with one of flat angry intensity. They stood this way for a moment, neither moving forward or back or dropping his eyes; then, slowly, the tautness gave way. The two men continued to look nowhere but at each other, but somehow the pitch had been lowered, and words were once more possible. It was Daniel who spoke first, and oddly enough his tone was almost conversational.

"Well," he said, "I'll say this for you. For someone who doesn't talk a hell of a lot, you do pretty good once you get going."

Tom shook his head; he seemed tired. "I said too much," he said. "A lot more than I wanted to say. I'm sorry."

"No no," Daniel said. "That's all right." His voice was abstracted; he looked around him, seemingly with no clear idea of exactly what he was looking for. He continued to look very slowly and carefully: a comprehensive survey. His eye stopped on the suitcases at the foot of his bed. He walked and tentatively lifted one. Tom moved over as if to help him, but his father waved him off.

"No no," he said. "I was just getting the heft of it. Billy and the pals will be here in a few minutes anyways." Once more, he looked all around the room very slowly. "Well," he said, finally, "there we have it. Oh yes. Well . . . it's a nice room I've got out there at the Smiling Valley, Tom? I think you said it was a nice room."

Tom said, "It's a nice room, Dad." He felt exhausted; he also felt ashamed. Yet at the same time he was somehow glad that he had said what he did; he would not have taken the words back. They had been necessary to him. . . .

"That's good," Daniel said. "A nice room. Plenty of size? Plenty of light? That's what counts most with me, Tom: the light. I hate a dark room. I dunno why. I always did. Even when I was a little boy. And then later, of course, when I was traveling all over, I had my share of them. And more than my share. I remember one time I was playing Liverpool. Liverpool, England. Thirty years ago now, it must be. No, thirty-five. Because that was the time I was there with the Winston Trio and Charlie Lacasse. A good act. They're all dead now, I think, except maybe Billy Winston. And I'll tell you who else was on the bill: Vesta McGuire. A homely girl, about the size of a hydrant. From New Zealand. She had a split throat or something; anyways, she could sing in two voices at once. "Listen to the Mocking Bird," "When the Dew Is on the Rose at Dawning" — that kind of thing. Not a class act, you know, but all right: the people liked her. Oh yes, I . . . what was I talking about now, Tom?"

"The room," Tom said. "In Liverpool. It was dark."

"Dark!" Daniel said. "Dark's not the word for that room, Tom. I've been in dark rooms in my time, but I never saw the like of that, before or since. You'd come home from the theater, you know, in the afternoon, and outside the sun would be shining, but inside that room it'd be like midnight. On account of the window, you know. There was only one, and that was a fake. It opened into a closet. Oh no, Tom, that was an awful room. Dark. That's why I hope this one is good and light."

"There's plenty of light, Dad," Tom said. He remembered his talk with Brother Martin; he added, "Four windows: it's a corner room."

"A corner room!" Daniel said. "Ah, that's nice. A corner room. Plenty of air, you know: it comes at you from all sides. And light as well. That's what I always liked about this room I had here. It was always cool, and it was always light. You couldn't beat this room on a hot day, or a dark one either." He looked around him once more, taking in the premises fondly. "But I don't have to worry about that, do I? Or anything else. It's all settled now. Yes. Did I thank you, by the way, for saying you'd take care of all the bills out there?"

Tom said, "That's all right, Dad."

"The thing is," Daniel said, "it could all mount up to a pretty penny in the end. Places like that, you know, they don't give you anything for nothing. It could come to a hell of a lot of money, Tom!"

Tom said, "That's all right, Dad. We'll take care of it."

"Although," Daniel said, "I don't suppose it will come to so much, at that. I mean, at my age, how the hell many more payments can you make? You pay in advance, I suppose?"

"Yes," Tom said shortly. "It doesn't make any difference, Dad." He was not eager to prolong this line of conversation.

"Yes, well, you would," Daniel said, musingly. "Those places, you know, they take no chances. Do they bill you by the week or month, I wonder? Which one, Tom?"

Tom said, "I don't know . . . it really doesn't matter, Dad."

"Oho!" Daniel cried. "That's where you're wrong: it damn well might matter! I'd get it by the week, if I were you. I mean, otherwise you might put down a whole month's worth the first of some month, and after only a couple of days — bango! *Then* try to get your money back! I tell you, Tom, I know those places. They can have more priests and nuns than doorknobs, all saying prayers together, but just try to get a penny back from them! Just try that sometime!"

"Yes, well, we're not worrying about that, Dad. Now look: why don't you. . . ."

"Oh yes," said Daniel, waving all this away, "I know all about those places. And I know about money, too, Tom. I may not have a hell of a lot today, but there was a time I had enough. Not that I was a millionaire, you know, or anything like that, but I was always well paid. And I was always in demand. So I had a bit put by. But it went. I dunno how, exactly: I never was what you could call a wild man. Or even a sport. But it went. What with one thing and another, it went. Schools, you know: they're very expensive."

Suspicion flicked in Tom; he looked sharply at his father, but the old man went on without looking at him and without pausing.

"I don't say it was *only* schools, of course. It was other things as well." He added thoughtfully, "I suppose. But anyways, it went. Or most of it did. There's still some people around that owe me a good bit, here and there. Actors mostly, you know. If any of it ever comes through, I'll pay you back. By God, I can't tell you when you'll get it, though!"

Tom said firmly, "Look, Dad: it's not important. It really isn't. So forget about it, will you?"

"Not important, Tom?" Daniel said. "Not important? Well, maybe it isn't. Not now. No no, not now. Well. . . ." And now, once again, he took a long slow look around the room, and came back at last to his son. "So here we are," he said. "Well . . . I guess this is where we say goodbye to each other. Isn't that right, Tom?"

Embarrassed by the moment, Tom said, "I guess it is. For a while anyway, Dad."

"For a while." Daniel seemed to consider this. "Well," he said, "the only thing is, Tom, I never knew you hated me. I never knew that."

"No," said Tom, shaking his head. "I don't hate you, Dad."

Daniel did not respond to this. "I knew, of course, that we weren't *pals*," he said. "But, I mean, how the hell could we be that? I didn't have

[203]

some job like a grocer or a banker that kept me
at home. My job was different. I was always away
a good bit."

Tom said flatly, "Yes."

"So I was never what you might call your chum,
exactly," Daniel said. "The way some Dads are.
I knew that. But I thought to myself, 'Well, all
right, we're not as close as we might be, maybe,
but still and all, we're friendly enough. And why
shouldn't we be? I'd never hurt him. I'm the boy's
father, and he's my son.' That's what I thought,
Tom. I never in God's world thought, 'Well, here's
my son that hates me.' "

"You've got it wrong, Dad," Tom said. "I don't —"

"All right," Daniel said, interrupting again, "I
might not of been there every blessed minute while
you were small. I don't say I was. I had to travel
around, like I said. But does that mean I forgot
you? I don't think it does. I remember all the little
things I used to send you from different places
I went to. For your birthday, maybe, or if I wasn't
going to be home at Christmas. I remember I used
to wonder sometimes if there was a boy in the
whole United States that got the stuff you did
from all over. Little toys, you know, from Canada
and India and Ireland and Mexico and places like

that. Nice toys, you know. Oh, they might not of cost a fortune, but you wouldn't get toys like that around here. And then not only the toys, but the stamps that would be on the packages! All kids save stamps, Tom, and who got more stamps from all over than you? And who was the one that sent them to you? Hey? Oh yes, you know the answer to that one, all right. I dunno, a Dad that does that, maybe he might not get home every night to read bedtime stories about Bunny Rabbit Goes to the Blueberry Dump, but he does something else. Something else that the other Dads didn't do. So I dunno about hating a Dad like that, Tom. I suppose that's why I was so surprised."

It was a long and, to Tom, an exasperating speech; it brought him back to his earlier impatience. He said, "About those presents: all those toys. I remember them. And I remember what —"

But here he stopped again and shook his head. "No," he said, "I don't want to go into *that*. That won't take us anywhere. All I want to do is make one small point: I don't hate you, Dad. I don't exactly feel like giving three cheers for you — you've probably gathered that — but *I do not hate you.*"

"Well, that's all right, Tom," his father said in

a mild voice. "Whatever you want to call it. It's no great matter now anyways, is it? It's all in the past. And I don't suppose we'll be seeing too much of each other from tonight on. You realize, Tom, that I couldn't stay here now. I mean, even if you wanted me to stay, I couldn't. I wouldn't feel right. Not after what's been said."

"We've both said too much," Tom said. "I don't think it would be very comfortable."

"There's some things you can't forget, you know," Daniel said. "Even though you think you can. I might start out all right, with us being nice as pie to each other. And then one night I might just be sitting here, reading, maybe, or thinking, and all of a sudden I'd remember what was said to me. And I'd feel bad. I wouldn't want to do that, Tom. Or else you might be in bed some night, talking to the wife, you know, and all of a sudden you'd start thinking about me. And things I'd done. Like the schools I sent you to. Or maybe not the schools: I notice you don't like to think about them. But maybe about the presents, the little things I used to send you from everywhere. And then *you'd* feel bad. . . ."

"That sounds fair," Tom said. "Let me get this straight, now: you'd remember what I did wrong, and you'd feel bad. And I'd remember what I did wrong, and I'd feel bad. And everything comes out even, right?" He stared at his father, the returning irritation mixed with a curious respect. "You know, in a way you're marvelous," he said. "No matter where you are, you can always slip right back into Let's Pretend. Now you're the man in charge of the gift counter. Look out, everybody, here come some more presents! I've got only a few left, I gave so many to my son!"

"I see, Tom," Daniel said. "So now I didn't give you any presents. So now I'm a liar as well as everything else: is that the way the wind blows?" His voice grew louder. "Don't try to pull that stuff on me, Tom! I won't take it from you or anybody else. Nobody's ever called Waltzing Daniel Considine a liar and got away with it. You got those presents and you know damn well you did!"

"Oh, I got them, all right," Tom said. "I told you: I remember them well. I remember every present you ever gave me — which, just for the record, is no great trick. You talk as if you were some kind of roving F. A. O. Schwartz: toymakers all over the world practically peed their pants whenever you blew into town: 'Hurry up, Max, here comes Mister Santa Claus!' Isn't that the pitch, Dad?

[207]

More or less? Wherever you were, whatever you did, you never forgot your Sonny Boy! Those gifts kept pouring down: I should have worn a helmet to shelter me from the rain! Well, there *were* presents — but I didn't need any helmet, and I didn't have to duck. They were few in number, Dad — damn few. And very very far between. You talk about my birthday — that's a laugh. You never remembered my birthday in your life. You don't even know when it is, do you? Can you come within a month of it? I'll bet you can't. I'll bet you fifty dollars, right now, that you can't!"

"Oh by God, there it is again!" Daniel cried. "The lawyer talking! Where did you go, what did you do, when did it happen: tell it all to me right down to the last second! Names, dates, places: that's what matters to you! Not a word about the presents, except 'Why didn't you give me more?' "

"Then let's have a word about those presents, if that's what you want," Tom said swiftly. "You know what I remember best about them, Dad? None of them ever seemed to have been bought in an honest-to-God *store*. They always arrived handsomely gift-wrapped in old newspapers, and laid out in some cheesy, leftover container for something else. But that didn't matter, did it, because when you shucked all the trimmings and got down to the real red meat inside, the presents themselves — well now, what red-blooded American boy wouldn't feel his heart beat just a little faster when he held in his own two hands a genuine cheap plaster Toby jug? Fully two inches high and all the way from Merrie Olde England! Or that pair of perfectly matched jumping beans that arrived — slightly dead — from south of the border, down Mehico way? Or how about that special leather dishrag that came in from Canada one year? I *think* it was a dishrag: no one could figure what else it could possibly be. Actually, some of the kids on the block thought that even as my presents went this was a fairly crappy one, but then I pointed out to them that it said 'Welcome to Manitoba' right on it, and might very well have been chewed into its present condition by a real live Eskimo! Oh, I tell you, Dad, those were *toys!* And when you think, not so much of the presents themselves, but of what lay *behind* them: the thought, the planning, the weeks of careful selection — well, by George, Dad, you can hardly trust yourself to speak! No kidding! In fact about the only thing I can do right now is to ask you a question. One simple question: a question that's been bothering me for a long time."

He looked steadily at his father now, and the

fierce, jeering note left his voice; he said, "Did you ever once, just once, give me anything that you didn't pick up at the last minute at some lousy souvenir counter in a railroad station? When you were between trains and had a couple of hours to kill and absolutely nothing else to do and so out of sheer boredom you remembered that another year or so had rolled around and wasn't it high time you sent another piece of junk to young What's-His-Name? Your son?"

"By God Almighty, I see now why you're so quiet all the time!" Daniel shouted. "Oh yes! It's because when you do start to jabber you give yourself away! You can't stop yourself: the whole big college boy front peels off, and what's underneath but the same old cold, greedy kid! I tell you this: I'm glad you said what you did! I'm glad I found you out at last! I knew you hated me, but I never knew why. And now I do. Oh yes! I see now what I did that was so damn wrong! I see where I made one hell of a mistake with you: *I forgot to give you Cadillacs!*"

The weariness that Tom had felt before now came over him again, all at once and stronger than ever. He had said things he had never said before, that he had held within him all his life, but now, instead of feeling that this had been important or necessary, he felt that it had been useless. He felt drained and blank: it seemed to him that nothing he had said had made the slightest impression on his father, and that anything further, whether whispered, shouted, or merely spoken, would make none either. His father and he did not meet and could not meet; all this bitter talk was wrong and had no point; he felt that unless he stopped now it could go on all night, and all to no purpose at all. And so he said, "No. No dice, Dad. We're not picking up that ball again. We've had enough. If you think I hate you — well, then you think I hate you. And if you think those presents were the big thing, that they really mattered — well, then you go right ahead and think that, too. But I'm done. I've had my say. It hasn't done any good. For either of us. I'm sorry, Dad. No more speeches tonight."

"By God I know one thing," Daniel said, looking about him wildly. "I can't wait to get out of this house!" He walked over to his suitcases, and stood over them. "I wish to hell Billy would get here. Then you'd see the last of me in short order. Not that that would break your heart!"

But Tom did not reply. He was as good as his

word: the argument was over. He did not leave
the room, but walked to his former position by the
window and, as before, stood looking out into the
night. Daniel watched him and waited; nothing
came. He sat on the foot of his bed; after a moment he began to tap the floor restlessly with one
foot: it was the old early morning noise, but now
Tom did not even hear it. Daniel spoke, but now
in a low, grumbling tone, almost to himself.

"I never thought I'd see this day. I never thought
I'd see the day when I'd be tickled to death to say
goodbye to this house. By God, all the time I was
away — in the last couple of years, at least — all
I thought about was coming here and staying here.
In my own boy's house. With my own boy. And
now I can't wait to go. To see the last of it. And
him."

Tom, still looking out the window, gave no sign
of having heard any of this; he did not move. And
Daniel, at this point, seemed to be looking for no
response. He gazed downwards, towards the floor,
his eyes appearing to be fixed on nothing in particular. He seemed to be speaking entirely to himself.

"So I'll go to this place," he said. "The Smiling
Valley. Good God, what a name! But name or no

name, it'll be like all the rest. You move in — and there's nothing but strangers around. You get sick — and there's nothing but strangers around. And you die — and there's still nothing but strangers around. All right. What the hell do I care. It's still better than being sneered at and yelled at and laughed at and hated. By my own son. And why? What for?"

And now he seemed gradually to have shifted — to be talking not exclusively to himself. In the lift of his head, in the shift of his eyes towards the window, there was perhaps the bid for a reply. If so, the bid was disappointed. Tom remained silent.

"What did I do that was so bad?" Daniel asked. His voice was puzzled; he seemed to be saying: *I am now asking reasonable questions that require a reasonable answer.* "What did I do? I'll tell you one thing I did. I paid for everything: doctors, hospitals, clothes, food, schools. My God, all those schools! But you went through them all right and no arguments from me. You're an educated man and a lawyer today — and you're that because I paid. But now I'm told that doesn't count: that's not one of the things that matters. It's like the presents: they don't matter either, do they? They're something you make fun of, have a good laugh at with your friends. Well, all right, maybe they weren't the greatest presents in the world — I never knew what kids liked, anyways. But at least I gave them to you — is that so bad? Is that something to hate a man for? And there we have it: I gave you things, I paid the bills, I made you what you are. And all the while there was something else: something you seem to of forgotten. In all your life, I never laid a hand on you, or said a cross word to you. So then, what did I do to you that was so wrong? What the hell did I do to you that was wrong *at all?*"

And this was not a hint, a subtle bid — it was in fact a command for an answer. It got none. Tom stood at the window, neither moving nor speaking. Daniel watched him sharply, anxiously, and when the silence persisted, he started to speak once more, changed his mind, and then gazed down at the floor again. He seemed to be debating with himself, almost struggling; he lifted his head to say something, then stopped before he had said a word. The struggle went on; it came to an end very quickly as he suddenly looked up at his son's back and said, very loudly, "ALL RIGHT! I LEFT HOME! I LEFT YOUR MOTHER! AND I LEFT YOU!"

And at this, Tom stirred at last. He closed his eyes; then, slowly, he turned from the window to face his father.

"*That's* what you were waiting for, isn't it?" Daniel cried. "*That's* what you've been wanting me to say all along! *That's* something that matters, hey? *That's* something that counts!"

Facing his father completely now, Tom said slowly, "Yes. That counts, Dad."

"All right, all right!" Daniel said. He was on his feet now, speaking very quickly, as if speed were all-important, his greatest ally. "I know, I know! I know everything you're going to say! But remember this, Tom! Remember this: you don't know the whole story! It's not all one-sided, oh no, not by a long shot! Remember that, Tom, before you start in!"

But Tom did not start in. It was the first time that his father had ever admitted the fact of his desertion; it was the crack in the wall; Tom, watching his father carefully, had the feeling that the talk had suddenly moved to another level, that at any moment now he might hear something which was somehow terribly important to him. He waited, saying nothing, and Daniel raced along.

"Oh yes! I left, I ran away, so I'm to blame:

that's the story you got! Isn't that right, Tom? But what about my side of the story? Hey? What about that? I had my reasons, I can tell you that! I'll say nothing against someone who's not here to defend herself — that's not my style — but *I had my reasons*. Good reasons! Now: what d'ye say to that?"

But Tom said nothing. He still looked at his father, his face expressionless. And Daniel did not wait for words: intent on what he was saying, he rushed forward in his monologue.

"Yes, reasons!" he cried. "Plenty of them! Did you ever know this, Tom: *I was never appreciated in my own house?* Nag, nag, nag, scrapping all the time: it was no Home Sweet Home for Waltzing Daniel Considine, I can tell you that! You didn't know that, did you, Tom? Oh yes, if I left home, I had plenty of reasons, and don't you forget it!" He stared combatively at his son, then said, "You don't believe that, do you? Oh, you don't have to tell me: I have eyes in my head, I can see. I see the look you're giving me, but let me tell you this: *you're wrong*. Whatever you're thinking, you're wrong! I know what you're thinking — and it's a terrible thing to be thinking about your own father! You're looking at me and you're thinking: *There stands a selfish bastard*. You're thinking that all along the line I didn't want to be bothered. You're thinking I got tired of having a wife and child with me all the time. You're thinking I got fed up with coming home to the same setup day after day when I could of been traveling around all the cities of the world in great style. You're thinking I always hated being a family man, and so one day I said the hell with it all, and up and left. That's what you're thinking, Tom: isn't that right? Well, let me ask you this: did you ever think the real reason I left was something else? That maybe I left because it was better that I did? Better for everybody, not just me. Better for your mother. Better for *you*. Did you ever think of it that way, Tom?"

It was not a question which moved Tom. He stood looking at his father in the same silent, curiously expressionless way as before. This time Daniel waited, but when nothing was forthcoming, he began to talk again, but now flatly, without the hectic animation, the rush of his previous speeches.

"Well, your mind's made up, I can see that," he said. "No one's going to change that for you, hey? No matter what they say? You know who's to blame, and that's that. Well, all right. What the hell do I care, anyways?"

He looked at Tom sullenly. Tom returned the look, although without altering his own calm and rather disquieting absence of expression. The two men stood in this way for a long moment, and it was Daniel who broke this by turning and walking away. He walked slowly until he reached the wall at the head of his bed. There, facing the wall, his back to his son, he spoke again, but this time a new note had entered his voice: it was the note of partial compromise, of slightly grudging concession.

"Over forty years ago," he said. "It's a hell of a while to remember who did what and why. All right. I'm a fair man. I don't say it was all her fault. Not a hundred per cent. I might of been partly to blame. *Partly.* I don't say I was a saint; I don't say I never did wrong. I might of said little things or done little things that got on her nerves now and then. But a man on the stage like myself, an actor, sometimes he's got a little temperament. That's what makes him different from other people. Your mother never understood I was different, Tom. She never understood that Waltzing Daniel Considine wasn't like some of these bums around here that left the house the same time every morning and came back the same time every night after

selling meat or underwear or insurance all day
long. She never understood me, Tom: the kind of
man I was, or what I did. She even used to laugh
about my public! My fans! She had a tongue like
a razor, Tom, and if you never felt it, it was because she used it up on me. And if I'd stuck around
and listened to her and been the kind of a stick-in-
the-mud she wanted me to be, do you know what
would of happened? I'd of hung up the old shoes
for good: *there would of been no Waltzing Daniel
Considine.* That's what would of happened, Tom,
sure as you're born. So you see, what the hell could
I do? I had no choice, I had to go. You can see
that now, can't you?"

He had turned to face his son halfway through
the explanation; now he looked at him urgently,
obviously wanting some sign of approval. But
there was none; there was no sign at all but the
steady, unchanging look which Daniel found increasingly unsettling.

"What the hell do you want from me, anyways?"
he said. "I said it might of been partly my fault,
didn't I? What more can a man say? That it was
all my fault? Or mostly my fault? When it wasn't?
By God, it wasn't! What I did I damn well had to
do! For the good of everybody! It's as plain as the

[219]

nose on your face. Put yourself in my shoes just for once, Tom. Put yourself there and ask yourself this question: Could I of done anything else?"

Once again it was an appeal, but Tom still waited for what had to come, and Daniel, because he had to, and because there was now nothing else to do, went doggedly on.

"That's some answer, isn't it? Not even a nod of the head. Well, you don't have to answer: I know what you'd say anyways. I can read you like a book. *I could of stuck around a little longer:* isn't that the way it goes, Tom? Isn't that what you want me to say? Well, all right, maybe I could of. I don't know what the hell good it would of done, but maybe I could of. And maybe when I went away *I could of come back more often than I did:* is that it, too, Tom? Well, all right there, too. Maybe I could of. I don't say for sure I could, but maybe I could. And then once I did get back I could of stuck around for longer times, maybe had little vacations with you — isn't that what's on your mind? Standing there looking at me like some damned judge! Who the hell ever gave you the right to judge your father, that's what I'd like to know? Oh yes, Tom, I see right through you! I know what you'd like me to say. Just to make you feel good, to make you feel as though what you're doing is right. And so I'll say it for you: *All right. Maybe I could of done all that.* Just maybe. There! Now, are you satisfied!"

But clearly Tom was not satisfied, for he went on looking at his father as steadily as ever. And Daniel, now more uncomfortably aware of this than ever, started to speak, then stopped. He started again — and stopped. Then, just as he had done earlier, he turned away from his son and stood facing the wall, as if what he had to say needed this partial privacy. Tom watched him very closely now; he felt that what he was waiting for was about to come at last. Daniel seemed right on the point of committing himself, yet something was holding him back. Again there appeared to be the interior struggle; Tom sensed the tension in the old man. It was a tension which collapsed suddenly as, almost with a sigh of relief, Daniel capitulated.

"All right," he said, in a low voice. "All right all right all right. No maybes, I *could* of. I could of. More than that, I . . ." And here he hesitated, there was just the beginning of a final and very brief struggle; then, at last, he gave in all the way. "I *should* of. I should of, I should of."

And to this Tom responded. His eyes closed for just an instant; his whole body seemed to relax. Daniel slowly turned around, and this time Tom looked at his father in a different way: more personally, without the even judging stare. But Daniel now seemed not to be concerned with this; he went on talking in a private way, again seemingly for his own benefit.

"I dunno how it all happened, anyways," he said. "It's all so long ago. One thing led to another, I suppose, and then, one day . . . well, I just decided the hell with it. I just decided I'd get out. So I quit, Tom. I quit on your mother. And I quit on you. That was a bad thing to do. I'm sorry."

Tom said, "All right, Dad." There seemed to him to be not much else to say. Or nothing that he could think of. Daniel had said everything; his son was not quite sure what he could say or do now. . . .

"I went off when I shouldn't of," Daniel said slowly, "and I didn't come back when I should of. That's about the size of it, I guess. Oh, I thought about coming back, many's the time, but then I'd stay away, and the longer I'd stay, the harder it'd be to come back. So I didn't. Can you understand that at all, Tom? No, don't answer: why should you? I didn't come back, and that's that. Why the hell should you hear a lot of excuses. They aren't any good, anyways. All I can say is I'm sorry. It's too late, I know that, but I say it anyways."

And Tom said nothing because he still did not know what to say. This new, contrite Daniel left him strangely uneasy: uneasier than at any previous point in their talk. He suddenly felt that although he had heard what he had wanted to hear, that although he had, in a sense, *won*, in another sense he was in a curious position of disadvantage.

"So I didn't come back," Daniel repeated. "Except every once in a while, you know. And then when I did I got out again damn quick. And that was bad too, of course. I dunno why I did it, exactly. I suppose it was the dancing, as much as anything else. I was always a dancing man, Tom. All the years I danced I never got tired of it. I never got tired of any part of it. I dunno if you can understand, Tom, but to come running out on the stage, you know, and hear everybody in the place start to clap their hands as soon as they catch sight of you — oh, I tell you! You don't forget a thing like that, Tom. And you don't get tired of it. Oh yes, I always loved the dancing!"

"No argument there, Dad," Tom said. "You

loved dancing, all right." And even as he said this, he felt it was unfair, but Daniel did not seem to hear.

"I dunno why I'm telling you all this," he said. "It doesn't show me up any better, does it? If I loved dancing so much, where does that leave me as a family man, hey? And yet, you know, Tom, here's a funny thing: I always thought of myself as a family man. Specially in the last couple of years, most of the time all I thought about was coming back. I dunno why that should be, but anyways, that's the way it was. All I got thinking about, day after day, was coming back here to my own home town. And specially to you, Tom. You were the only family I had left."

"Well, not quite," Tom said. "There's Delia."

"Delia," Daniel said. "Ah well, Delia's my sister and all that, but no man could think of Delia as *family*. No no. No, all I thought about was coming here. Wasn't that a funny thing, Tom? After all that happened? Wasn't that funny?"

"Well . . . you came, Dad," Tom said, feeling more uncomfortable than ever. "And you were with us. For a good while. And even now, you won't be a million miles away."

Daniel said, "Yes, well, that's as may be. Anyways, I dunno why I'm talking this way now. I know it's damn late in the day, Tom, but I just want to say again I'm sorry for any harm I did you."

Tom said quickly, "All right, Dad."

"Forgive and forget, Tom?" Daniel said.

"It's all right, Dad," Tom said. It was not quite a direct reply, but Daniel gave no sign of being aware of this.

"By God, I dunno what the hell you felt about me over all the years," he said. "I dunno that I want to know. I knew you didn't like me much. I can't say I blame you. And I'll tell you something else, Tom. A couple of times this last year, while I was up in the room here, I asked myself why you were letting me stay in the house as long as you did. I knew you really didn't like me, and I knew the wife didn't. So I asked myself: Why? What for?"

"Never mind that, Dad," Tom said. It was embarrassing; he said, "It's all in the past; why go over it again?"

"No no, wait, Tom," the old man said. "Wait. I want to tell you this. So I asked myself: Why? After what I've done to him? And then one day, Tom, I thought of something. I remembered that one of the times I came back home — oh, it must be nearly twenty-five years ago now — you were in college: I dunno in what year. Anyways, the reason I was home was I was booked here: to play a week at the Bijou. And I gave you tickets: you and two of your college chums. I dunno that you even wanted to come, Tom, but they did. So you came. Do you remember that, I wonder?"

Tom said, "Yes. I remember."

"Was that the first time you'd ever seen me on the stage, Tom?" Daniel asked. "I think it was. Anyways, I did my act, and afterwards you came backstage to say hello. You and your chums. And we talked for a couple of minutes. I wanted to ask you out to dinner, the three of you, but you said you had to go. You were in a big hurry, Tom. So we only had a couple of minutes. And so I sat there, with the makeup still on, you know, and all of a sudden I noticed something about you. Do you know what it was, I wonder?"

Tom said quickly, "No. It was a long time ago."

"Yes, a long time ago," Daniel agreed. "But I remember it, Tom. I remember that when I looked at you, sitting there in my dressing room with your two chums, I saw you were ashamed of me." He looked at Tom gravely now, and Tom, for the first time in this encounter, did not meet the look squarely. "Did you know I saw that, Tom?" the old man continued. "I did. I saw you were ashamed of me, not on account of what I might of done to you or your mother, but because I was an actor. A dancer, making his money by doing foolish steps and falling down on the stage. And you know, I looked at your two chums sitting there beside you. They were dressed no better than you: I remember thinking you all looked like peas in a pod. You might almost of been brothers. But the way I remember it, one of them had a Dad that was a big shot on the Stock Exchange, wasn't that it? And the other had a Dad that kept horses and was head of one of the big banks. And there they sat: two nice, clean, high-class young fellers with two nice, clean, high-class Dads. And there you sat: like them, you know, but with a different kind of Dad. And so you were ashamed. Or anyways that's what I thought you were. Was I wrong about that, Tom?"

It was one of those moments when to lie, even to evade, somehow was impossible. For the first time since his father had come back, Tom was ashamed before him; he knew that he had reddened, and slowly he looked at him directly and said, "I guess it's my turn, isn't it? I'm sorry, Dad. It's a little late for me, too, but . . . I apologize."

"Ah well, that's all right," Daniel said mildly. "The only thing was, I thought maybe that was why you let me stay on, even though you didn't like me much: you felt a little guilty about what you did."

"No," Tom said. "The truth is, I'd forgotten it. I really had. Until you brought it up just now. It's not exactly the kind of memory I'd want to hold on to."

"No no, of course not," Daniel said. "A man would want to forget something like that: that's only natural. And I forgot it myself, you know. It took a little time. When a man sees his own son is ashamed of him — well, the sting lasts a bit. But it's all gone now. And I forgive you, Tom. Why not? You're my only boy. And it's all long ago. No, what's done is done, you're sorry for what you did to me, and I'm sorry for what I did to you. And there we are." He looked at Tom with a little smile. "By God, I said we never talked to each other. But we fixed that tonight, I guess."

"Yes," Tom said. "We did that, all right."

"Well, it was damn good we did," Daniel said. "It cleared things up, you know. It's a damn shame

[228]

we didn't have more talks like this before."

"I don't know," Tom said, more cautiously. "I have a hunch one talk like this might be about all the traffic would bear."

"Well, I didn't mean just like this, of course," Daniel said. "That wouldn't do at all, would it. No, what I mean is something different." He spoke now with a growing enthusiasm. "What I mean is, to talk man to man: that's a great thing, Tom. By God, here I am, almost at the end of the line, and for the first time I get the feeling I can talk with my own boy, and he can talk with me. That's a good feeling, Tom. Knowing we're all squared away with each other. It's a hell of a time to have no more talks, Tom! Just when we find we can talk to each other!"

"We'll talk, Dad," Tom said. He was less ebullient than his father; also, something in the old man's speech had touched off a faint spark of wariness again. He said, "After all, you'll be around; you're not going to the moon."

"I dunno know about that," Daniel said. "As far as talk goes, I might as well be. You know what they say: out of sight, out of mind. There's a lot of truth in that, Tom. No, we can't do it that way. I was thinking of something else." Visibly, now, his enthusiasm began to mount; he leaned eagerly towards his son. "Here's what I was thinking, Tom: let's scratch the whole thing off and start off fresh! Hey? Wouldn't that be a great thing? All right, you said some bad things to me, I said some bad things to you: we'll forget them! And I'll tell you what I'll do, Tom: *I'll stay here.* Here in the house! The hell with the Smiling Valley and all my plans: they're not important when it comes to my own boy! No, I'll stay here with you. Only it'll be different this time! You'll see, Tom! A boy and his Dad, all squared away now, knowing each other for the first time, talking to each other like . . . well, like real *pals!* The way they should of in the first place!"

Tom had listened to the first few words without quite comprehending; then, very quickly, he understood, and slowly he began to shake his head. Daniel, intent on what he was saying, did not at once see this.

"Oh yes!" he said. "Forgive and forget and start out all new! That's the nice way to do things! And the wife! There's the wife, of course! We can't forget her, can we? And we won't forget her. She'll go along nice as pie, once she sees how happy you are, Tom! Happy once more with your old Dad,

the way it should be! Oh yes, I . . . well, what's
the matter?" he said, with sudden sharpness.
"What's the matter with you there, shaking your
head like that?"

"No," Tom said. "It won't work, Dad. It was a
good try, but it won't work."

"*What* won't work?" Daniel said. "What the hell
are we doing, playing games at a time like this?
By God, I don't understand you at all! What's
wrong now?"

"Tricks," Tom said wearily. "You're full of tricks,
Dad. One a minute, every minute. The whole thing
from first to last was a trick. Well, no dice. Goodbye, Dad."

He moved towards the door; Daniel cried, "Wait!
Wait wait wait! In God's name, what's the hurry?"

At the door Tom stopped; he turned and said
only, "I'll let your friends up when they come. And
I'll see you downstairs before you go."

"Good God Almighty, boy, come back here!"
Daniel said, in an agonized voice. "All right, all
right, I tried to soften you up a bit: what's wrong
with that? I'm an old man! I'm your *father!* Forgive and forget: isn't that what we said, Tom?
Remember? All I want is to be friends! To be here

in the house and be friends! Pals, Tom, pals! That's all I want!"

"I know what you want, Dad," Tom said. "But we settled all that four weeks ago."

"Oh God, I'm wise to you!" Daniel said, his voice changing. "I see it all now. You don't want me around because I'd remind you of something! Something you did that was so cheap you'd give half your life to forget it! But how can you forget it if I'm here in the house, hey? If I was here you'd remember it day after day: the big college boy that was ashamed of his Dad in front of his fancy friends! And if it wasn't for his Dad putting him through such good schools he never would of met friends like that in the first place! That's why you're throwing me out on my arse, Tom! That's why! You're afraid I'll remind you for the rest of my days!"

"Wrong," Tom said. With his hand on the door-knob, he faced his father. "All wrong. That happened, yes. It happened once. It happened twenty-five years ago, and I'm ashamed of it. But I'm not that ashamed, Dad. You're going out of here — or rather, you're not staying here any more, which-ever way you want it — because in one part of my life you didn't give a damn about me or about your wife, and because in another part of my life you still don't give a damn about me or about *my* wife. I was almost going to say you never gave a damn about anyone or anything, but then I remembered that wasn't true. You actually did have two great loves in your life, Dad: Vaudeville, and You. Well, Vaudeville's dead — but you've still got You. So keep the old love affair going, but don't expect any help from me. I was never any part of it, and I'm not going to be now!"

He opened the door to leave; Daniel shouted, "Oh by God, you won't save yourself by this! Oh no! You won't put me out of your head that easy! You won't be able to forget, I'll see to that! I'll . . . I'll . . . I'll *telephone*, that's what I'll do! I'll telephone you every day from the Smiling Valley! I'll telephone you *night* and day! You'll never know when it's coming! You'll hear a ring, you'll pick up the phone, and it'll be me: 'Hello: this is the Dad you were ashamed of in front of your snobby friends! Aren't you proud of yourself today!' That's what you'll hear, Tom, and that's what the wife will hear, every day until the day I die!"

Then, very quickly, he changed; his voice dropped and softened; his face, red and raging, became pleading; he said, "Or else, Tom, it can be like I said? Pals, Tom? Here in the house? The two of us? And the wife, of course? There's still a chance, hey? A Dad and his boy? Pals?"

Tom looked for what seemed like a very long time at his father. It was as if he wanted to say things that would now not be said, and that would be of no use even if they were said. When he did speak, he said only four words.

"I'm sorry, Dad," he said. "Goodbye."

He looked at his father for perhaps a second more; then, swiftly, he left the room, closing the door behind him.

"Day and night!" Daniel shouted. "Night and day! You'll never forget! I won't let you! By God I won't!"

He stood facing the closed door as he shouted, his fist raised, his old body shaking. He stood there for some time after his son had left. At last he turned, still fuming. He looked all around him, surveying his surroundings exactly as he had done a hundred times that day; this time there was no satisfaction in what he saw, and the very act of turning seemed to lose him the support of his fury. When at last he stopped he looked small, miserable, and alone. He walked slowly to a chair and plopped down; he buried his face in his hands.

He remained in this position a few moments, then raised his head and shouted again.

"Damn damn damn damn! Damn them all to hell!"

There was a knock on the door. Daniel paid it no attention; the knock was repeated, and through the door he heard his sister Delia's voice.

"Daniel?" she said. "I know you're in there, Daniel!"

"Oh good God!" he cried. "Go away!"

Delia opened the door just wide enough to stick her head in. "I'm going, Daniel," she said. "I'm on my way. Two of the brothers out to the Smiling Valley were coming into town and they were nice enough to give me a ride. And on the way I remembered you, Daniel. The way I always do. That's the way I am. Well, anyways, we're all outside now, Daniel: right outside the door. We'll give you a ride out if you'd like. You and all your stuff. It's a station wagon, Daniel: there's plenty of room for you and your bags."

"Get the hell out of here, Delia," said Daniel. "You and the brothers both!"

"Isn't that nice, Daniel!" she said. "Isn't that typical! Well, it's no more than I expected from you. You think you're high and mighty now, just

[235]

because they gave you a corner room. Oh, I heard
all about it. I heard all about it from Mrs. Arthur
B. Maguire. 'Well, Delia,' she said to me, 'I suppose
you heard about them giving your brother room
three-oh-four. There's plenty of people around here
have been waiting for Mrs. Cass to die so's they
could get to that room! Some of them have been
waiting a long long time! And now what do they
do but pass them all up and give it to a newcomer!
They gave it to your brother!' Oh, I can tell you,
Daniel, you're not the most popular man in the
world out at the Smiling Valley now. Oh no! I —"

"For the love of God get out of here!"
Daniel cried.

"All right, I'm going," she said. "There's some
people just won't be helped, that's all. I won't even
say goodbye, Daniel. After all, I'll be seeing you
tomorrow at the Valley. We'll be seeing a lot of
each other from now on, I imagine. We spent our
whole lives apart, Daniel, and now at the end
where do we wind up but side by side at the Smiling Valley! It's just like a fairy story, Daniel —"

But Daniel jumped out of his chair now and
advanced towards the door; Delia's head disappeared, and the door slammed. Daniel stood at the
door for the second time in minutes, quivering

with frustration and rage. This subsided, and he walked slowly back to his chair, where he slumped down deeper in despair then before. Out of habit he gazed all around him again, staring miserably at the four walls; there was no comfort there. He rose and paced nervously about, but this did not console him. Desperately, he tried to think, to plan; this did no good. And, at last, the old man was faced with the fact that he was stuck, that he had come to the end of his resources, that he had no more tricks left to play. In short, there was no way out; his face, his bearing mirrored this feeling.

Then, suddenly, he stopped: one last possibility occurred to him. It was not a congenial possibility, and he was even a little timid and reluctant to approach it. But he had tried everything else, and so now, slowly, self-consciously, looking about him almost as if, although alone in the room, he were afraid of being observed, he began to get down on his knees. This descent, which began slowly, accelerated as a kind of panic overtook him, and in the end he really *threw* himself into the position of prayer and started to speak hurriedly even before he was ready.

"Name of the Father the Son and the Holy

Ghost," he mumbled, perfunctorily blessing himself. "Oh my God, I . . . all right, I know I haven't
been the best man in the world. I could of done
better, you don't have to argue with me there. I
know that. I'm sorry for that. I'm very very sorry
for that. And I know I've done a lot of things I
shouldn't of done, I know, I know. I was busy, you
know, always away on tour, but all the same
I should of done better, I know that! But here's the
point, here's what I'm getting at: I *will* do better.
I'm *going* to do better: that's a promise! If only
you can do something for me now, I swear I'll do
anything you want me to! *Anything!* I'll say a
ton of Hail Marys! Every day! I'll go to Mass! All
the time! I'll give some money to charity, to
churches. I'll . . . I'll . . . well, I'll do a lot better, you'll see! Only, dear God, get me out of this
one! Do something with the boy! Soften him up!
Get him back in here so's he'll tell me I can stay!
That's what I'm asking you for! Work on him, dear
God! Get him back in here! You can do it if you
want, I know you can! Do it and I'll never forget
you! Only do it *fast!* Whatever you do, do it fast
or I'm a goner! Dear God, I'm here on my knees
asking you! Don't you hear me? *I'm on my
knees. . . .*"

[238]

And then, suddenly, unexpectedly, he heard the sharp sound of a knock on his door. It was a loud, authoritative knock, the knock of someone in a hurry. Daniel stopped, startled. He looked at the door, unable to believe what he had heard; he spoke in a voice filled with wonder and incredulity.

"*Tom?*" he said. "Is that you, Tom?"

But it was not Tom.

"Open up, Daniel!" a loud, buoyant voice called. "Open up, my dear man!"

Slumping, Daniel closed his eyes. "*Oooh,*" he groaned. "Oooh, good God!"

"Hail hail, the gang's all here," Billy called cheerfully. "Father, Gottlieb and myself. Ready and waiting for the good news! Open up, my dear man!"

Daniel could not immediately speak; when he did, it was to himself.

"I might of known," he said bleakly. "I might of known."

Very slowly, he got to his feet, and as he did, he addressed himself to the ceiling, completing his prayers.

"*You're just like all the rest,*" he said.

Wearily, he took a couple of steps toward the

door, then stopped. He thought for a moment, shook his head as if to clear it, then shrugged and spoke.

"All right, Billy," he said. "I'll be with you in a second."

He went dispiritedly over to the bureau, where he stood looking at himself in the mirror. It was not an encouraging sight; he did not care. He had no great urge to improve his appearance. But in the last few seconds he had determined what would have to be done, and so, almost by instinct alone, he began the old business of preparing himself for a performance. He smoothed back his hair, slapped color into his cheeks, patted his clothing into place, inhaled and exhaled deeply. He stood smartly erect and tried an experimental smile; he moved his feet in the beginnings of a dance step. Then he stopped, re-examined himself, and shrugged again. He crossed to the foot of his bed and picked up his record player; he plugged this into an outlet, and from a folder took a record which he placed on the turntable. Miserably, he stood by the machine, waiting for the music to come up.

"Daniel!" Billy cried through the door. "Are you lost in there? Let us in, my dear man? We're all ready for the celebration!"

Each word was a blow; Daniel shut his eyes tight. "Oh good God, good God, good God," he whispered. After a moment he opened his eyes and said with great false heartiness, "One second now, Billy. I'm just getting things ready! I've got a little surprise for you when you come in! One second now!"

The music started to come up. Daniel listened to it, buried his face in his hands once more, then lifted his head and turned the volume up full: it was his theme song.

"Come in!" he cried. The music was very loud now, and was approaching the chorus; Daniel got ready. "Come in, come in!"

And as he called out to them, he began to dance, twirling his way from the foot of the bed over to the windows. The door opened and the three men entered, Father Feeley in the lead. They stopped abruptly at the sight of the old figure dancing around the newly stripped room. They stared at him; all together, they looked at each other, bewilderment in their eyes. Still dancing, never breaking stride, but keeping his face away from them, Daniel continued moving swiftly in a great circle.

"Come in, come in!" he cried, his voice filled with a desperate gaiety. "It's all a part of the surprise! D'ye know why I'm dancing? I'll tell you why: I'm dancing for joy! Because I finally made up my mind! Oh yes! I've got great news for you! The thing is this: I've changed my plans! Oh yes, that's what I've done: *I've changed my whole plans. . . ."*

The three men came slowly forward as Daniel danced on, shouting over his shoulder. Now they were looking, not at their old friend, but at each other, and the bewilderment in their eyes was now mixed with pain. They thought they knew what had happened; they wondered what would, what *could,* happen next. . . .

And for the first time in a great many years Daniel, still dancing, still shouting, wondered this too.

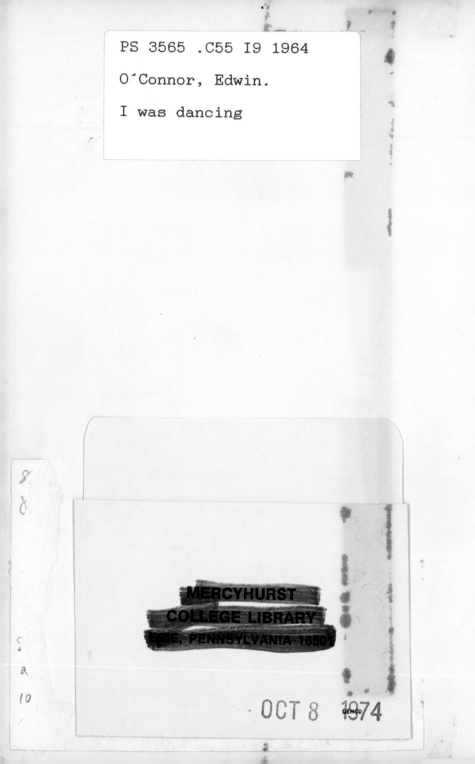